Love in the Shadow of the Full Moon

Matt Philip

Published by Bright Minds Books, 2024.

This is a work of fiction. Similarities to real people, places, or events are entirely coincidental.

LOVE IN THE SHADOW OF THE FULL MOON

First edition. September 21, 2024.

Copyright © 2024 Matt Philip.

ISBN: 979-8227231727

Written by Matt Philip.

Table of Contents

Description

Love in the Shadow of the Full Moon is a tale of magic, mystery, and self-discovery.

Elera embarks on a journey to restore the balance between light and shadow, guided by the moon's magic and the enigmatic Kairos, a protector with secrets of his own. Together, they must face illusions, confront their fears, and battle the shadow lurking within the moon's light. With the fate of their world at stake, their bond is tested as they navigate the fine line between trust and betrayal.

This is a story of love, sacrifice, and the fight to protect what truly matters.

Dedication

To those who seek the light in the darkest of times, and to the dreamers who never stop believing in the magic within themselves. This is for the ones who face their shadows and continue walking, even when the path seems uncertain.

May you find the strength to embrace both the light and the dark, knowing that love and trust will always guide you home.

Preface

The journey of *Love in the Shadow of the Full Moon* was born from a fascination with the balance between light and darkness, and how both are essential in shaping who we are.

The moon, with its ever-shifting phases, became the perfect symbol for this exploration—its light a beacon in the night, its shadows a reminder that even in darkness, beauty can be found. Through Elera's story, I wanted to delve into the complexities of love, fear, and sacrifice, while also creating a world rich with magic and wonder.

This book is not just about adventure but about the choices we make when faced with the unknown, and how we navigate the shadows of our own hearts.

Chapter 1: The Glow of the First Full Moon

The village of Hallowvale was nestled in the valley between two towering hills, where the trees whispered ancient secrets, and the streams sang songs of times long past. It was a peaceful place, where the rhythms of life were simple and predictable. But for Elera, the world felt full of mysteries, especially when the full moon rose high in the sky. On those nights, her heart raced with a longing she couldn't quite explain. There was something about the silvery light that called to her, as if it held the key to an adventure she had always dreamed of.

One such night, the full moon hung above the village like a glowing pearl, casting shadows and lighting up the world in a soft, magical hue. Elera sat by her window, her chin resting in her palms, her eyes fixed on the moon. She could hear the faint rustle of leaves outside, the gentle wind brushing through the tall grass, and the distant hoot of an owl. It was all so peaceful, yet her thoughts buzzed with restless energy.

"Elera, it's late. You should be asleep," came the familiar voice of her older brother, Seren, from the next room. His tone was gentle but firm, as always.

Elera didn't budge. "I'm just watching the moon. I'll go to sleep soon, I promise."

Seren sighed. "You always say that. I don't know why you're so fascinated by it. It's the same moon every month."

But to Elera, it was never the same. Each full moon felt different, as though it carried a new secret or a new story waiting to be uncovered. Tonight, though, something felt especially different. The pull of the moon was stronger than ever, almost as if it were beckoning her.

Once Seren had gone to bed, Elera quietly slipped out of her room and crept down the wooden stairs of their cottage. She grabbed her cloak from the peg by the door and fastened it tightly around her shoulders. The air outside was cool, and the sky was clear, with stars scattered like tiny jewels around the glowing orb of the moon.

Without a second thought, Elera made her way toward the hills beyond the village. She had always wanted to see what lay beyond the familiar boundaries of Hallowvale, and tonight, the moon's glow felt like an invitation. Her footsteps were light, barely making a sound as she crossed the grassy fields, her eyes fixed on the hills in the distance.

As she climbed higher, the village behind her grew smaller, its lights fading until they were just tiny dots against the darkness. The higher she went, the brighter the moon seemed to shine, as if it were guiding her. Elera's heart pounded with excitement and a hint of nervousness. She had never ventured this far from home before, but she felt no fear. Something deep inside her told her she was exactly where she needed to be.

After what felt like hours of climbing, Elera reached the crest of the hill. She stood there, catching her breath, and gazed out at the landscape below. The view was breathtaking. Rolling hills stretched out as far as the eye could see, bathed in the soft glow of the moonlight. A silvery mist clung to the ground, giving the scene an otherworldly quality. It was as though she had stepped into a dream.

But then, something caught her eye—a figure, standing at the edge of the hill, looking up at the moon. Elera's breath hitched in her throat. Who else could be out here at this hour? She hesitated for a moment, wondering if she should turn back. But her curiosity got the better of her, and she slowly approached the figure.

As she drew closer, she could make out more details. The figure was a boy, slightly older than her, dressed in a dark cloak that seemed to blend into the shadows around him. His hair was wild, dark, and unruly, and his posture was still, almost as if he were part of the night itself.

Elera cleared her throat softly, unsure of how to announce her presence. "Hello?" she called, her voice barely above a whisper.

The boy turned slowly to face her, his dark eyes glinting in the moonlight. For a moment, neither of them spoke. Elera felt an odd sensation, as though she had known this stranger her entire life, even though she had never seen him before.

"You shouldn't be here," the boy said, his voice quiet but firm, like the wind through the trees.

Elera blinked, startled. "I could say the same about you," she replied, trying to sound braver than she felt.

The boy studied her for a moment longer before turning his gaze back to the moon. "The full moon isn't what it seems," he said cryptically. "It holds secrets. Old ones. Dangerous ones."

Elera frowned, intrigued despite the warning. "What do you mean? Everyone knows the stories about the moon, but they're just legends. Tales to entertain children."

The boy shook his head. "They're more than that. The moon is powerful. It watches over everything, and not always for the better."

Elera stepped closer, her curiosity piqued. "How do you know all this? Who are you?"

For a moment, the boy didn't answer. He seemed to be weighing something in his mind, his eyes never leaving the moon. Then, finally, he spoke. "My name is Kairos. I've been watching the moon for a long time. It has brought me here... and now, it has brought you, too."

Elera's heart skipped a beat. "Why me? I'm just a girl from the village. What does the moon want with me?"

Kairos turned to face her fully now, his expression serious. "The moon calls to those who are meant to see beyond the ordinary. It chooses those who can understand its magic. And tonight, it chose you."

Elera stared at him, unsure of what to say. The idea that the moon had chosen her for some kind of special purpose was thrilling, but also overwhelming. "What happens now?" she asked, her voice barely a whisper.

Kairos smiled faintly, though there was something sad in his eyes. "Now... we follow the moon's light. There's a path it wants us to take, and only by walking it will we understand what it's trying to show us."

Elera glanced up at the moon, its glow brighter than ever, casting long shadows across the hills. She didn't know what lay ahead, but something inside her told her that this was just the beginning of a much greater adventure. With one last look at her village far below, she turned back to Kairos and nodded.

"Then let's follow it," she said.

Together, they stepped into the moonlit night, their journey just beginning.

Chapter 2: Kairos and the Moon's Secret

The cool night air surrounded Elera and Kairos as they walked down the other side of the hill, the full moon lighting their path. Despite the mysterious and somewhat somber words of her new companion, Elera's heart raced with excitement. It was the first time she had ventured beyond the familiar limits of her village, and now she was walking with someone who seemed to know secrets about the moon—secrets that she had only dreamt of.

The silence between them stretched on for a while, but Elera couldn't hold back her questions any longer. She glanced at Kairos, who was walking beside her with a calm, almost graceful stride.

"So," she began, hesitantly, "you said the moon chose me. What does that mean? How can the moon choose anyone?"

Kairos didn't answer right away. His gaze was fixed ahead, his dark eyes focused on something unseen. When he finally spoke, his voice was quiet but certain. "The full moon has always been more than just a light in the sky. It's connected to the world in ways most people can't see. There are ancient forces at play—forces of love, balance, and sometimes danger. The moon knows who can understand its magic, and it draws them in."

Elera frowned, trying to understand. "But I've never done anything special. I've just... always liked the full moon. It feels different somehow, but I never thought much of it."

Kairos glanced at her, a small, enigmatic smile playing on his lips. "That's where it starts. It draws you in, makes you feel things you can't explain. That's how it was for me."

Elera raised an eyebrow. "And how long have you been following the moon's call?"

Kairos stopped walking for a moment and looked up at the sky, the silver light casting his face in sharp relief. "A long time," he said softly, almost to himself. "Longer than you'd believe."

Elera's curiosity deepened, but she didn't press him. Instead, she focused on the path ahead, which was leading them deeper into unfamiliar territory. The hills seemed to rise and fall endlessly, and in the distance, the outline of a dense forest loomed. Elera shivered slightly, though she wasn't sure if it was from the chill in the air or the unknown journey ahead.

After walking in silence for a few more minutes, Kairos finally broke the quiet. "I need to tell you something important," he said, his tone suddenly more serious. "The path we're on isn't just a simple adventure. There are dangers—things the moon doesn't show to everyone. And there's a choice you'll have to make before this journey ends."

Elera felt a knot form in her stomach. "What kind of choice?"

Kairos looked at her, his expression unreadable. "It's different for everyone. But it always comes down to understanding what the moon is really asking of you. It's not just about following the light; it's about what you're willing to give up to understand its magic."

Elera's heart skipped a beat. "Give up? Like what?"

Kairos turned his gaze back to the moon. "Sometimes it's something small. Sometimes it's something bigger. But the moon always asks for something in return. Love, sacrifice, trust—those are the things it tests."

The idea of giving up something, especially something as precious as love or trust, unsettled Elera. She had always been curious about the moon's mysteries, but she had never considered that there might be a cost.

As they walked, the trees of the forest loomed closer, their branches casting long, twisted shadows across the ground. The forest looked ancient, as though it had been there since the beginning of time, untouched by human hands. Elera had heard stories about these woods—stories of creatures that lived in the darkness, of strange lights that flickered between the trees, and of people who ventured inside and never returned.

Kairos seemed unfazed as he led the way toward the forest's edge. "The moon's path leads through the woods," he said calmly. "There are things you need to see inside."

Elera hesitated. "Are you sure? I've heard stories about these woods... bad stories."

Kairos nodded. "The forest is old, and like the moon, it holds its own secrets. But there's nothing here that will harm you if you understand the rules."

"Rules?" Elera asked, her brow furrowing. "What kind of rules?"

Kairos smiled slightly, his expression softening for the first time. "Just one, really. Trust the moon's light. Don't let fear blind you to what it's trying to show you."

Elera took a deep breath and nodded, though her heart still pounded in her chest. With one final glance at the moon above, she followed Kairos into the shadowy depths of the forest.

The trees were tall, their twisted branches stretching up toward the sky like skeletal fingers. The moonlight filtered through the gaps in the leaves, casting strange patterns on the forest floor. As they walked, Elera felt a strange sense of both wonder and unease. The air was thick with the scent of earth and moss, and every sound—whether it was the rustle of leaves or the distant hoot of an owl—seemed amplified in the quiet of the woods.

Kairos walked ahead, his steps light and sure, as though he had traveled this path many times before. Elera followed closely behind, her eyes scanning the shadows for any sign of movement. She couldn't shake the feeling that they were being watched.

After what felt like hours of walking, they reached a small clearing in the heart of the forest. In the center of the clearing stood an ancient tree, its bark silver and shimmering in the moonlight. The tree was unlike anything Elera had ever seen before—it was as if the moon itself had touched it, leaving behind a trace of its magic.

"This is where it begins," Kairos said quietly, stepping closer to the tree. "The moon's power is strongest here. If you listen closely, you'll hear it."

Elera frowned, unsure of what he meant. She took a few tentative steps toward the tree, her heart racing. The air around the tree felt different—charged, almost electric. She closed her eyes and focused, trying to hear whatever Kairos was talking about.

At first, there was only silence. But then, slowly, a faint sound began to emerge—a soft, melodic hum, like the distant ringing of a bell. It was barely audible, but it was there, resonating deep within the tree.

Elera opened her eyes, her breath catching in her throat. "What is that?"

Kairos smiled faintly. "The moon's song. It's what calls to those who can hear it. It's what led you here."

Elera stared at the tree, her mind racing. She had never heard of such a thing before—never imagined that the moon could sing, or that its magic could be felt in such a tangible way.

"Why can I hear it?" she asked, her voice barely above a whisper.

"Because the moon has chosen you," Kairos said softly. "And now, it's your turn to decide whether to follow its call."

Elera looked at Kairos, her heart pounding. She had always dreamed of uncovering the moon's secrets, but now that she was here, standing on the edge of something far bigger than she had ever imagined, she wasn't sure if she was ready.

"What if I don't want to follow it?" she asked, her voice trembling slightly.

Kairos' expression grew serious. "That's your choice. But if you turn back now, you may never understand what the moon was trying to show you. And you'll always wonder what could have been."

Elera bit her lip, her mind racing. She didn't know what lay ahead, but something inside her—something deep and unshakable—told her that she couldn't turn back now. The moon had called her for a reason, and she had to see this through.

Taking a deep breath, she nodded. "I'll follow it."

Kairos smiled, and for the first time, his smile reached his eyes. "Then our journey begins."

Chapter 3: The Night of the Star Blossoms

The ancient forest seemed to close in around Elera and Kairos as they walked deeper into its depths. The full moon's light flickered in and out, weaving through the trees and casting strange shadows on the ground. There was a sense of otherworldliness here, as though the forest existed on the edge of reality, where magic was real, and time flowed differently. Every rustle of leaves and crack of branches seemed to echo with unseen energy.

Elera's heart raced with a mix of fear and excitement. She wasn't sure what she had expected when she decided to follow Kairos and the moon's call, but this felt like the beginning of something incredible. Still, she couldn't shake the sense that they were being watched, though she couldn't see or hear anything unusual.

"Where are we going?" Elera asked after a while, glancing at Kairos. His face, lit by the dim moonlight, looked calm but distant, as though he were listening to something far off.

"To a place few people know about," Kairos replied, his voice barely above a whisper. "A place where the moon's magic is strongest."

Elera's curiosity deepened, but before she could ask anything else, something caught her eye. Up ahead, the trees began to thin, and a faint, glowing light spilled into the path. It wasn't the soft silver of the moonlight, but something more vibrant, more alive.

As they stepped into the clearing, Elera gasped. Before her was a sight unlike anything she had ever seen.

The clearing was filled with flowers—thousands of them—blooming under the full moon's light. They glowed with a soft, pale luminescence, their petals shimmering like stars that had fallen to the earth. The air was thick with their sweet, intoxicating scent, and the gentle breeze made the petals sway, as if the flowers were dancing in the moonlight.

"These are star blossoms," Kairos said, his voice soft with reverence. "They only bloom on nights like this, under the full moon. They're a sign that we're on the right path."

Elera stepped closer to the flowers, her eyes wide with wonder. The blossoms seemed almost magical, their glow casting a soft light that made the whole clearing feel alive. She knelt down and gently touched one of the petals, expecting it to feel delicate, but instead, it was cool and smooth, like polished stone.

"They're beautiful," she whispered. "I've never seen anything like them."

Kairos smiled faintly. "Few people have. The star blossoms are rare. They're said to be born from the light of the full moon itself. They hold a special kind of magic, but only those who can hear the moon's call can find them."

Elera looked around the clearing, feeling a sense of awe wash over her. The moon above seemed to shine brighter here, its light reflecting off the blossoms and casting the whole scene in a soft, ethereal glow. For a moment, she forgot about the dangers Kairos had warned her about. Here, in the heart of the forest, surrounded by the star blossoms, everything felt peaceful and perfect.

But that peace didn't last long.

A sudden rustling in the bushes nearby made Elera jump to her feet. She spun around, her heart pounding, and looked toward the source of the sound. Her eyes widened as a small creature darted out from the undergrowth, its body shimmering in the moonlight.

At first glance, it looked like a fox, but its fur wasn't the usual red or brown. It was a deep midnight blue, streaked with silver, and its eyes gleamed like tiny stars. The creature darted around the clearing with incredible speed, weaving in and out of the star blossoms, as if playing a game with itself.

"Silko," Kairos muttered, shaking his head. "I should've known you'd show up."

Elera blinked in confusion. "Silko? What... what is that?"

The creature suddenly stopped in front of them, sitting back on its haunches and grinning mischievously. "That's no way to introduce me, Kairos," the creature said, its voice light and playful. "I'm much more than just 'Silko.' I'm the fastest, most clever, and dare I say, the most charming creature in these woods."

Elera's jaw dropped. "It can... talk?"

The creature—Silko—gave an exaggerated bow. "Indeed, I can. But only to those who have been chosen by the moon, of course. It's a very exclusive talent."

Elera exchanged a bewildered glance with Kairos, who sighed in exasperation. "Silko is... well, let's just say he's a creature of the night. He knows the forest and its secrets better than most, but he's not exactly reliable."

Silko gave a mock look of offense. "Not reliable? That's hurtful, Kairos. After all we've been through together. I've saved you from more than one tricky situation, if I recall correctly."

Kairos rolled his eyes but didn't argue. Instead, he turned to Elera. "Silko tends to show up when the moon's magic is strong. He's unpredictable, but he might be able to help us."

Elera looked at Silko with a mixture of curiosity and amusement. The creature was unlike anything she had ever seen, and his playful demeanor made it hard to take him seriously. But there was something about him—something that felt connected to the moon's magic.

"So, what brings you here, Silko?" Kairos asked, crossing his arms. "You don't usually bother with star blossoms."

Silko grinned again, his sharp teeth gleaming in the moonlight. "I felt something interesting in the air tonight. And when I saw the two of you heading into the forest, I knew I had to come along. After all, I can't miss out on the adventure, can I?"

Kairos raised an eyebrow. "Adventure?"

Silko nodded enthusiastically. "Oh, yes. There's something brewing tonight. The star blossoms are a sign, but there's more to come. The moon is speaking louder than usual, and I have a feeling it's going to lead us somewhere important."

Elera felt a shiver run down her spine. There was something both exciting and ominous about Silko's words. She glanced at Kairos, who seemed to be considering what Silko had said.

"Do you trust him?" she asked quietly.

Kairos sighed. "Trust might be too strong a word. But Silko has a way of sensing things. If he says something's happening, we should pay attention."

Silko gave a mock salute. "I live to serve."

Elera couldn't help but smile at the creature's antics, despite the unease building in her chest. She looked around at the glowing star blossoms, feeling the weight of the night settling over her. The air felt thick with magic, and she knew that whatever lay ahead was going to be far more challenging than anything she had imagined.

"So," Elera said, turning to Silko. "If you're so clever, where do we go from here?"

Silko's eyes gleamed with mischief. "Ah, that's the spirit! I like you already, Elera. As for where we go... well, that depends on what you're looking for."

Elera frowned. "I don't know what I'm looking for."

Silko's grin widened. "Exactly. And that's what makes it fun."

Kairos stepped forward, his expression serious once again. "Enough games, Silko. If you know something, tell us."

The creature sighed dramatically. "Fine, fine. No fun with you, is there? Look, all I know is that the moon's magic is leading us toward the Hidden Peaks. The star blossoms are just the beginning. If you want to understand the moon's secret, that's where you need to go."

Elera's heart skipped a beat. "The Hidden Peaks? But that's... no one goes there. It's too dangerous."

Silko shrugged. "Dangerous? Maybe. Exciting? Definitely. But if you want to know the moon's true power, you'll have to face the danger."

Elera exchanged a glance with Kairos, who nodded solemnly. "The Hidden Peaks," he repeated. "It's where the moon's magic is strongest. If we're going to understand what the moon is trying to show us, we have no choice."

Elera swallowed hard. The thought of journeying to the Hidden Peaks filled her with both dread and excitement. She had always dreamed of adventure, but now that it was here, she wasn't sure if she was ready.

But there was no turning back now. With one last look at the glowing star blossoms, she nodded.

"Let's go," she said, her voice steady despite the fear gnawing at her heart. "To the Hidden Peaks."

Chapter 4: Seren's Skepticism

As dawn approached, the dense forest began to fade behind Elera, Kairos, and Silko. The three of them walked in silence, the moon retreating behind the horizon and the faint glow of the rising sun painting the sky with shades of pink and gold. After hours of walking under the eerie, moonlit glow, the warmth of the sun felt comforting. Yet Elera couldn't shake the feeling that she was now tied to the moon's secrets, its magic still humming quietly beneath her skin.

Silko darted ahead playfully, as if the journey to the Hidden Peaks was nothing more than a game. His midnight-blue fur shimmered under the fading moonlight, but now that the sun had started to rise, his form seemed to blur, and he faded in and out of sight like a living shadow.

"He'll disappear soon," Kairos said quietly, noticing Elera's gaze. "Silko can only stay visible while the moon is strong. He'll be back when night falls again."

Elera nodded, her mind still buzzing from everything they had seen the previous night—the glowing star blossoms, the strange melody of the moon's song, and the cryptic warnings from both Kairos and Silko. It felt like her world had expanded overnight, revealing hidden layers of magic and mystery that she had never known existed.

But as they emerged from the forest, the familiar sights of her village came into view. Hallowvale's thatched-roof cottages and smoke rising from the early morning fires reminded Elera of the life she had left behind for a night of adventure. Her heart clenched as she realized she had snuck out without a word to anyone, least of all her older brother, Seren.

"I should go home," Elera said, glancing at Kairos. "Seren will be worried."

Kairos nodded, though his face remained serious. "Go. But remember, we'll need to leave soon if we're to reach the Hidden Peaks before the next full moon. The journey won't be easy."

Elera nodded, feeling a strange pull between her duty to her family and the allure of the moon's mysteries. She hesitated for a moment before turning away from Kairos and Silko, who now looked like nothing more than a shadow in the fading light of dawn.

When she reached her cottage, the door creaked as she pushed it open, wincing at the sound. Inside, the familiar scent of fresh bread filled the air, and Seren was already up, sitting at the small wooden table with a plate in front of him. His sharp eyes immediately fixed on her, and Elera knew she wasn't going to escape the questions she dreaded.

"Where have you been?" Seren's voice was calm, but there was an edge to it.

Elera bit her lip and stepped inside, closing the door behind her. "I... I went for a walk," she said, avoiding his gaze. She wasn't ready to tell him about the moon's call, Kairos, or the magical journey she was now part of. Seren was always so practical, so grounded in reality. He wouldn't understand.

Seren raised an eyebrow. "A walk? In the middle of the night? You've never done that before."

Elera shrugged, trying to sound casual. "I just needed to clear my head. I couldn't sleep."

Seren studied her for a long moment, his eyes narrowing. "You're hiding something. You've been acting strange for weeks now, staring at the moon every night like it's going to reveal some grand secret to you."

Elera's heart skipped a beat. He had noticed. But instead of admitting the truth, she shrugged again. "I'm just curious about the moon, that's all."

Seren frowned and leaned forward, resting his elbows on the table. "Elera, the stories about the moon and its magic are just that—stories.

Legends passed down through generations to entertain children. There's no real power there. I don't want you getting lost in fantasies."

Elera's chest tightened. "But what if the stories are true? What if there's more to the moon than we know?"

Seren sighed and stood up, walking over to the window. The morning light streamed in, casting long shadows across the floor. "You're starting to sound like one of the village elders. They believe in those old legends, but that doesn't mean they're real. We live in the real world, Elera. The moon rises, the moon sets, and life goes on. That's all."

Elera opened her mouth to argue but stopped herself. Seren wouldn't believe her, not without proof. She glanced at the door, her thoughts racing. She didn't want to lie to her brother, but she also couldn't ignore the call of the moon and the journey she had started with Kairos. There was something powerful and undeniable about it, something that tugged at her very soul.

"I'm not saying the moon's magic is real," Elera said carefully. "But what if there's something out there that we don't understand? Something worth exploring?"

Seren turned to face her, his expression softening. "I get it, Elera. You're curious. You've always been that way. But I don't want you getting hurt because you're chasing after something that doesn't exist."

Elera swallowed hard. She could feel the weight of his concern, but it only strengthened her resolve. There *was* something out there, something that called to her every time the full moon rose in the sky. And now that she had begun this journey, she couldn't stop.

"I'll be careful," she said, her voice quiet but firm.

Seren didn't look convinced, but he didn't press the issue. Instead, he sighed and sat back down at the table. "Just promise me you won't do anything reckless."

Elera nodded, though she wasn't sure if she could keep that promise. The path she had chosen was far from safe, but it was one she had to follow.

After breakfast, Elera slipped out of the cottage and made her way to the hill where she had first met Kairos. Her heart raced as she spotted him waiting for her at the top, his silhouette framed by the morning sky. Silko was gone, as Kairos had predicted, but the sense of urgency remained.

"You're back," Kairos said as she approached, his voice neutral but laced with a hint of relief.

Elera nodded. "Seren doesn't believe in the moon's magic. He thinks it's all just stories."

Kairos didn't seem surprised. "Most people do. The moon's power isn't something you can see with your eyes. You have to feel it. But that doesn't make it any less real."

Elera glanced back at her village, a pang of guilt tugging at her heart. "Seren's worried about me. He thinks I'm chasing after something that doesn't exist."

Kairos placed a hand on her shoulder, his expression serious. "This path isn't easy, Elera. You'll have to make choices that others won't understand. But you've already felt the moon's call. You know there's something out there."

Elera took a deep breath and nodded. "I know. I can't turn back now."

Kairos smiled faintly, a glimmer of approval in his eyes. "Good. We have to reach the Hidden Peaks before the next full moon. That's where we'll find the answers."

Elera felt a surge of determination wash over her. The Hidden Peaks. The journey ahead would be long and dangerous, but she was ready. She had always wanted an adventure, and now, standing at the edge of the unknown with the moon's magic guiding her, she knew she was on the right path.

"We'll leave tonight," Kairos said, his voice steady. "The journey will be difficult, but if you trust the moon, it will guide us."

Elera glanced up at the sky, where the faint glow of the sun was beginning to push away the last traces of night. The full moon might be gone for now, but its power lingered, like a quiet hum in the air. And though her brother didn't believe, though the village might never understand, Elera knew she couldn't deny the call.

"I'm ready," she said, her voice filled with resolve.

Kairos nodded, and together, they turned toward the distant peaks, the unknown future stretching out before them, illuminated by the promise of the moon's light.

As the day passed and night approached once more, Elera found herself standing at the threshold of a journey that would change her life forever. And this time, she wasn't just a girl from a small village. She was part of something far bigger, something that shimmered with the light of the full moon.

She wouldn't stop until she uncovered the truth.

Chapter 5: A Path Beyond the Shadows

Elera's mind was a whirl of thoughts and emotions. The conversation with her brother Seren still lingered in her heart. She knew he didn't believe in the moon's magic, and his words echoed in her mind, sowing seeds of doubt. But the more she walked, the more she felt the pull of the moon guiding her steps. She couldn't turn back now. Something far more important than her fears awaited her, and she had to see it through.

Kairos walked silently beside her, his face unreadable. He seemed more focused, his gaze fixed on the horizon, where the distant outline of the Hidden Peaks loomed against the darkening sky. The mountains were still far off, but their jagged peaks jutted up into the heavens like sharp teeth, waiting for those brave enough to approach.

As night fell, the moon began to rise once more, casting its silver light across the landscape. It felt like a comforting presence, watching over them as they ventured into the unknown. But with the moonlight came the shadows, and the path they followed grew darker and more treacherous.

"We're entering the Shadow Valley," Kairos said, his voice low. "This is where the moon's light begins to falter. The shadows here are thick, and they'll try to lead us astray. Stay close."

Elera's heart skipped a beat. The Shadow Valley was a place she had only heard about in whispers. It was said that the valley was cursed, filled with dark magic that could confuse travelers and trap them in its endless maze of darkness. Few who entered ever made it out, and those who did were never quite the same.

Elera pulled her cloak tighter around her shoulders, her gaze darting to the shadows that seemed to move on their own. "What do we do if we get lost?" she asked, her voice trembling slightly despite her attempt to sound brave.

Kairos didn't hesitate. "We trust the moon. Its light will guide us, even when we can't see it."

The path ahead twisted and turned, leading them deeper into the valley. The trees grew taller, their branches thick and gnarled, blocking out much of the moon's light. Shadows stretched across the ground, long and twisting, as if alive. The air was colder here, and a low, eerie wind whispered through the trees.

Elera's heart pounded in her chest as they continued forward. She tried to focus on the sliver of moonlight that peeked through the dense canopy above, but the shadows seemed to close in around her, making her doubt each step. Every so often, she thought she saw movement out of the corner of her eye—dark figures shifting in the trees, just beyond the edge of her vision.

Kairos walked with purpose, his steps steady and sure. He didn't seem afraid of the shadows, and Elera drew strength from his calm presence. But as they moved deeper into the valley, the darkness grew thicker, and even Kairos began to hesitate.

"The shadows here are different," he muttered, more to himself than to her. "Something's not right."

Elera's breath quickened. "What do you mean?"

Kairos glanced at her, his expression tight. "This valley has always been a place of darkness, but the shadows are stronger tonight. It's as if they're being drawn to us."

A chill ran down Elera's spine. She glanced around, trying to see through the thick darkness. The trees seemed to press closer, their twisted branches reaching out like claws. The wind had died down, leaving the air still and heavy. And in the silence, she heard it—a faint whisper, like voices carried on the wind.

"Do you hear that?" Elera asked, her voice barely above a whisper.

Kairos nodded, his face grim. "The shadows are speaking. They're trying to confuse us."

The whispers grew louder, though Elera couldn't make out any words. It was as if the shadows themselves were alive, speaking in a language she couldn't understand. The sound wrapped around her, making her feel disoriented, as though the ground beneath her feet was shifting.

"We have to keep moving," Kairos said, grabbing her arm and pulling her forward. "Don't listen to the voices. They'll try to lead you off the path."

Elera nodded, but it was easier said than done. The whispers were growing louder, filling her mind with doubt and confusion. The path ahead was no longer clear, and the shadows seemed to stretch out like endless corridors, leading in every direction. The moonlight had all but disappeared, leaving them in near-total darkness.

Panic began to creep in. "I... I don't know where we're going," Elera said, her voice trembling. "What if we're lost?"

Kairos squeezed her arm, his voice steady. "We're not lost. We have to trust the moon, even when we can't see it."

Elera tried to focus, but the whispers in the darkness were relentless. They seemed to be calling her name, urging her to turn back, to leave the valley and abandon the path. Her heart raced, and for a moment, she considered it. What if Seren was right? What if this was all just a fantasy, a dangerous illusion?

But then, something inside her shifted. She remembered the star blossoms, glowing under the full moon's light. She remembered the strange, melodic hum she had heard in the forest, the song of the moon. The magic was real—she had felt it. And now, it was leading her through the darkness.

With renewed determination, Elera took a deep breath and nodded. "I trust the moon," she whispered to herself.

Suddenly, a faint glow appeared ahead of them, like a flicker of light in the distance. It wasn't the bright, silver light of the full moon, but it was enough to pierce through the thick darkness of the Shadow Valley.

Kairos noticed it too. "That's our guide," he said. "We have to follow it."

Elera didn't question him. She followed Kairos as he led the way toward the distant light. The whispers grew louder as they approached, as if the shadows were trying to stop them, but Elera focused on the light, letting it guide her steps. It grew brighter as they neared, pushing back the shadows and revealing the path ahead.

The valley opened up before them, and the oppressive darkness lifted slightly. The glow led them to the edge of a cliff, where they could see the Hidden Peaks in the distance, their jagged forms silhouetted against the night sky.

"We're close," Kairos said, his voice filled with relief. "We made it through the valley."

Elera let out a shaky breath, her heart still pounding. The shadows had tried to confuse her, to make her doubt the path, but she had trusted the moon's guidance, just as Kairos had told her. And now, they were one step closer to uncovering the moon's secrets.

As they stood at the edge of the valley, Elera felt a sense of accomplishment wash over her. The path had been difficult, and the shadows had been terrifying, but they had made it through. And though the journey ahead was still uncertain, Elera knew that she could face whatever lay ahead.

The moon hung high in the sky now, its light shining down on them like a beacon. And as Elera looked toward the distant peaks, she felt a strange sense of peace, as if the moon itself was reassuring her that she was on the right path.

Chapter 6: The Silver River

The jagged mountains loomed in the distance, their sharp edges cutting into the night sky like black shadows against the stars. The journey had been long, and although the Shadow Valley was behind them, the path ahead was still fraught with unknowns. Yet, despite the chill in the air and the fatigue that tugged at her, Elera felt more determined than ever.

Kairos, as always, remained silent and focused, his dark eyes scanning the landscape ahead. The moon was high in the sky, casting its silver light across the rocky terrain, but there was a new energy in the air—something different from the quiet, mystical presence of the moonlight. It felt almost like anticipation, as though the very land was waiting for something to happen.

It wasn't long before the terrain changed. The gentle hills and rough paths gave way to a narrow canyon, its walls towering above them. The shadows here were deep and long, and the moon's light barely reached the ground. The air was thick with moisture, and the sound of rushing water echoed off the canyon walls.

"We're close to the Silver River," Kairos said, his voice low but steady. "It's the next challenge we must face."

"The Silver River?" Elera asked, her curiosity piqued. She had heard stories of a river that shimmered like liquid moonlight, but she had always thought it was just a legend, a tale told to children around the village hearth.

Kairos nodded. "It's no ordinary river. The water is enchanted, and only those who are pure of heart can cross it safely. For others... the river can be dangerous."

A knot of unease tightened in Elera's stomach. "What do you mean by 'pure of heart'? How does the river know?"

Kairos glanced at her, his expression serious. "The river reflects what's inside you. If you carry fear, doubt, or darkness, the water will turn against you. But if you have trust and love in your heart, the river will guide you across."

Elera swallowed hard. She had faced shadows, uncertainty, and whispers of doubt in the Shadow Valley, but this was different. This was a test, and one she wasn't sure she could pass.

As they walked deeper into the canyon, the sound of the rushing water grew louder. The air was cool and damp, and the walls of the canyon seemed to close in around them, adding to the feeling of anticipation that hung thick in the air. Elera's steps slowed as the tension mounted, her heart pounding in her chest.

Finally, they reached the riverbank.

The Silver River was unlike anything Elera had ever seen. It flowed through the canyon like a ribbon of liquid light, shimmering and glowing with an ethereal brilliance. The water seemed to pulse with a life of its own, reflecting the moonlight in shimmering patterns that danced across the canyon walls. It was beautiful—hauntingly so—but there was an unmistakable power beneath its surface.

Kairos stepped closer to the edge of the river and knelt down, dipping his hand into the water. The silver liquid swirled around his fingers, leaving behind trails of light that flickered and faded. "The river knows," he murmured. "It sees what's in your heart."

Elera's breath caught in her throat as she stared at the river. She had never been one to doubt herself, but this place—this enchanted river—seemed to strip away her confidence. What if the river found something dark in her heart? What if her fears, her doubts, were too strong?

Kairos stood and turned to her, his expression calm but firm. "We have to cross, Elera. There's no other way to reach the Hidden Peaks. But you have to trust yourself."

Elera nodded, though her hands trembled as she stepped closer to the riverbank. She could feel the pull of the water, its silent call. The silver liquid flowed serenely, but beneath the surface, she sensed the challenge it posed.

Kairos went first. He stepped into the river without hesitation, his feet barely causing a ripple as he moved. The water responded to him, parting smoothly and allowing him to walk across without resistance. It was as though the river recognized him, accepted him.

Elera watched in awe as Kairos reached the other side and turned to face her. His expression was unreadable, but his eyes held a quiet reassurance. "You can do this," he called softly. "Trust the moon. Trust your heart."

Elera's pulse quickened. She took a deep breath, willing herself to stay calm. Slowly, she stepped into the water, her feet sinking into the cool, shimmering liquid. At first, the water was still, gentle around her ankles. But as she took another step, a wave of doubt washed over her, unbidden.

What if the river doesn't let me cross? she thought. *What if it senses my fear?*

The water stirred, swirling around her legs, growing agitated as her thoughts spiraled. She could feel the river testing her, probing her heart, and with each second that passed, her fear grew.

Kairos' voice broke through the haze of panic. "Elera! Stay calm. You have to believe."

Elera's heart raced. The river's current tugged at her legs now, pulling her back, as if it could sense the doubt that had taken root inside her. The silver water churned around her, growing more turbulent with every step she took.

I can't do this, Elera thought, panic rising in her chest.

But then, a memory flashed in her mind—the star blossoms glowing under the moon's light, the hum of the moon's song, the pull she had felt to follow the moon's path. She had come this far, trusting in the magic, trusting in something greater than herself.

The moon chose me, she reminded herself. *It brought me here for a reason.*

With a deep breath, Elera closed her eyes and let go of her fear. She focused on the moon above, the steady light that had guided her through the darkness. She thought of her brother Seren, of Kairos, and of the journey she had undertaken. The doubt in her heart faded, replaced by a quiet sense of peace.

When she opened her eyes, the water had stilled. The river no longer churned against her; instead, it flowed smoothly around her, allowing her to walk forward. Each step became easier, the silver water parting for her as she moved.

Chapter 7: The Tale of the Moonlit Grove

The Silver River was now far behind them, but its magic still lingered in Elera's mind—a reminder of the power within her that she was just beginning to understand.

They had been walking for hours when Kairos finally stopped at the edge of a vast, shimmering forest. The trees here were taller than any Elera had ever seen, their silvery bark glowing softly in the moonlight. Their branches reached up to the sky, and beneath the canopy, the air was filled with a soft, almost musical hum. It was as though the forest itself was alive with magic, and Elera felt a strange sense of peace wash over her as they approached.

"This is the Moonlit Grove," Kairos said quietly, his voice reverent. "It's a sacred place. The magic here is strong, and it's connected to the heart of the moon."

Elera's breath caught in her throat. She had heard of the Moonlit Grove in stories, but like so many things on this journey, she had never believed it was real. The elders of her village spoke of a place where the moon's power gathered, where ancient beings watched over the world, unseen by ordinary eyes. It was a place of mystery and wonder, and now she stood at its threshold.

"Why have we come here?" Elera asked, her voice barely above a whisper.

Kairos stepped forward, his gaze fixed on the glowing trees. "There's someone we need to meet. Someone who can help us understand the moon's magic." He turned to Elera, his dark eyes serious. "But be careful. The magic here is old, and it doesn't follow the same rules as the world outside."

Elera nodded, her heart pounding with a mixture of excitement and apprehension. She followed Kairos into the grove, the soft glow of the trees lighting their way. As they walked, the hum of the forest grew louder, filling the air with a strange, soothing melody. It wasn't quite like the song she had heard in the earlier part of their journey, but it had the same ethereal quality, as though the very air around them was alive with magic.

The deeper they went into the grove, the more surreal everything became. The trees seemed to shimmer with every step, and the ground beneath their feet felt soft, almost like walking on clouds. Elera glanced up, and for a moment, she thought she saw figures moving among the branches—ghostly shapes, flickering in and out of sight, their forms blurred by the silvery light.

"What are those?" Elera asked, her voice hushed.

"Spirits," Kairos replied softly. "They're part of the grove's magic. They watch over this place, protecting it from those who don't belong."

Elera's skin prickled with unease, but she forced herself to keep moving. The spirits didn't seem hostile, but there was something otherworldly about them, something that made her feel small and insignificant in the face of the grove's ancient magic.

Finally, they reached a clearing in the center of the forest. In the middle of the clearing stood an enormous tree, far larger than any of the others. Its trunk was thick and gnarled, its bark glowing with a soft, silvery light. The branches spread wide above them, creating a canopy that seemed to hold the very sky in place. And at the base of the tree sat a figure—a woman, her hair long and silver, her eyes closed as she leaned against the tree's massive trunk.

Elera stared in awe. The woman looked almost like a part of the tree itself, her skin pale and glowing, her presence serene and timeless. She seemed to radiate an aura of calm, and Elera felt an overwhelming sense of reverence wash over her as they approached.

Kairos knelt before the woman, his head bowed in respect. "Runa," he said softly. "We've come for guidance."

The woman, Runa, opened her eyes slowly, and when she looked at them, Elera felt as though she were being seen not just on the surface, but deep within—her thoughts, her emotions, her very soul laid bare.

Runa's eyes were the color of the moon, a soft, luminous silver, and they held a depth of wisdom that made Elera feel both comforted and unnerved.

"You've traveled far," Runa said, her voice as soft as the wind through the trees. "And yet your journey is only beginning."

Kairos nodded, his expression serious. "We seek to understand the moon's magic. We need to know what lies ahead."

Runa's gaze shifted to Elera, and for a moment, she said nothing. Elera held her breath, feeling the weight of the ancient being's attention. Finally, Runa smiled—just a small, soft smile, but it was enough to ease some of Elera's tension.

"The moon's magic is not something that can be easily understood," Runa said, her voice gentle but firm. "It is the magic of love, of balance, of the unseen forces that bind the world together. To understand it, you must first understand yourself."

Elera frowned slightly, unsure of what Runa meant. "Understand myself?"

Runa nodded. "The moon's light reveals what is hidden in the shadows of our hearts. It shines on both the light and the darkness within us, showing us who we truly are. Only when you understand what lies within can you hope to grasp the moon's true power."

Elera felt a shiver run down her spine. The moon had already tested her once—at the Silver River, where she had faced her doubts and fears. But it seemed that was only the beginning.

"There is more you need to know," Runa continued. "The moon is not just a guide. It is a force that connects all things. Love, in its purest form, is the essence of the moon's power. But love is not always easy. It requires trust, sacrifice, and the willingness to face the darkness within."

Elera's heart skipped a beat. The idea of love being tied to the moon's magic made sense in a way she hadn't fully grasped before. But Runa's words also filled her with a sense of unease. What sacrifices would she have to make? What darkness would she have to face?

Runa's gaze softened as she looked at Elera. "The path ahead will not be easy. You will be tested in ways you cannot yet imagine. But know this: the moon's light is always with you, even in the darkest moments. Trust in it, and it will guide you."

Elera swallowed hard, feeling the weight of Runa's words settle over her. She had already faced shadows, doubts, and the enchanted waters of the Silver River, but she knew that the challenges ahead would be far greater. And yet, despite the fear gnawing at her, she felt a spark of hope. The moon's light had brought her this far, and it would continue to guide her, even when the way seemed impossible.

Kairos stood, his expression calm but resolute. "Thank you, Runa," he said, bowing his head in gratitude. "We will take your words to heart."

Runa smiled softly. "Go now, and remember: the moon's light is a reflection of what is within you. Let it guide you, and you will find the answers you seek."

Elera and Kairos bowed in thanks and turned to leave the grove. As they walked away from the great tree, Elera felt the weight of the ancient magic all around them, the hum of the forest vibrating through her very bones.

When they reached the edge of the Moonlit Grove, Elera glanced back at the glowing trees, feeling a strange sense of peace and purpose. The grove had revealed something important, something she hadn't fully understood before: the power of the moon wasn't just about magic or mystery—it was about the connections that bound all living things together. Love, trust, sacrifice—these were the true forces behind the moon's light.

Kairos glanced at her as they stepped out of the grove and back into the moonlit night. "Are you ready for what's next?" he asked quietly.

Elera took a deep breath and nodded. "I am."

Together, they walked into the night, the Moonlit Grove fading behind them. The path ahead was uncertain, and the challenges they would face were unknown, but Elera knew one thing for sure: she would follow the moon's light, no matter where it led. And with each step, she felt herself growing stronger, more confident in the journey that lay ahead.

Chapter 8: A Gift from the Moon

The grove's lingering magic still pulsed faintly in the air, a reminder of the ancient wisdom shared by Runa. Elera's mind buzzed with Runa's words: *Love, trust, sacrifice—the true forces behind the moon's light.*

Elera glanced at the sky. The full moon hung overhead, bright and watchful, casting its silver light over the mountains. The sight filled her with a strange sense of peace, but also a quiet unease. The journey ahead would be far from easy, and Runa's words about facing the darkness within herself had struck a deep chord. What sacrifices would the moon demand from her? What hidden truths would she have to confront?

Kairos, as always, walked silently beside her, his gaze fixed on the path ahead. He seemed lost in thought, though his expression remained as unreadable as ever. Elera had come to trust Kairos during their journey, but she couldn't help but wonder about the secrets he kept. The moon's magic flowed through him, but there was something about his quiet, distant demeanor that suggested he had faced challenges of his own—challenges that had left scars, whether visible or not.

After several hours of walking, the path began to narrow as they climbed higher into the mountains. The air grew colder, and the sound of the wind whistling through the rocks echoed around them. Elera shivered, pulling her cloak tighter around her shoulders.

"We should stop for the night," Kairos said, glancing at her. "There's a cave not far from here. It'll give us some shelter."

Elera nodded, grateful for the suggestion. Her legs were aching from the long trek, and the idea of resting—even for a little while—was more than welcome.

They continued walking until they reached the mouth of a cave nestled into the mountainside. The entrance was narrow, but inside, the cave opened up into a spacious chamber, its walls lined with shimmering crystals that reflected the moonlight from outside. It was beautiful, in a rugged, untouched way, and Elera couldn't help but feel a sense of wonder as she stepped inside.

Kairos began gathering dry wood from the nearby brush to start a fire. While he worked, Elera wandered deeper into the cave, her eyes drawn to the glittering crystals embedded in the stone. The crystals seemed to pulse with a soft, rhythmic light, almost as if they were alive, resonating with the same magic that flowed through the moonlit night.

As she ran her fingers lightly over the smooth surface of one of the crystals, a sudden, sharp pulse of energy shot through her hand. She gasped, stumbling back in surprise. The crystal seemed to glow brighter for a moment, and then, from deep within the stone, a faint hum began to fill the air. It was a familiar sound—the same melodic hum she had heard when she first encountered the star blossoms.

The moon's song.

Elera's heart raced as she listened to the sound, mesmerized by the gentle rhythm that echoed through the cave. It was as if the moon itself was speaking to her, calling out to her through the crystals. She knelt down, her gaze fixed on the glowing stone, and closed her eyes, letting the song wash over her.

Suddenly, there was a shift in the air, and Elera felt a strange sensation in her chest—like a tug, deep inside her heart. When she opened her eyes, she saw something lying at the base of the crystal. It was small, round, and glowing faintly with a soft, silvery light.

A moonstone.

Her breath caught in her throat as she reached down and picked it up. The stone was cool to the touch, but it pulsed with a quiet, steady energy. It felt almost alive, as though the moon's magic had been captured and condensed into this tiny, perfect object.

Kairos appeared at her side, his eyes widening slightly as he saw the moonstone in her hand. "A gift from the moon," he murmured. "You're meant to have it."

Elera looked up at him, her voice barely a whisper. "But why? What does it mean?"

Kairos studied her for a long moment before speaking. "The moonstone is a powerful talisman. It's a part of the moon's magic, and it will protect you on your journey. But more than that... it will guide you when the path becomes unclear."

Elera turned the stone over in her hand, marveling at the way it seemed to glow brighter when she touched it. "Guide me how?"

"The moonstone reacts to danger," Kairos explained. "When someone is in peril—when the darkness is near—it will glow, brighter and brighter, until it leads you to where you're needed most. It's a symbol of trust and love. The moon doesn't just guide us—it brings us together, helps us protect those we care about."

Elera stared down at the stone, her mind racing. A sense of awe washed over her as she realized what the moon had entrusted her with. The stone was more than just a magical object—it was a responsibility, a promise that she would face the challenges ahead with courage and compassion.

She closed her fingers around the moonstone and nodded. "I'll keep it safe."

Kairos smiled faintly, though there was a hint of sadness in his eyes. "It's not about keeping it safe, Elera. It's about using it when the time comes. The moonstone will show you the way, but you have to be willing to follow its call."

Elera swallowed hard, the weight of his words sinking in. The moonstone was a tool, but it was also a test. It would light her path, but only if she had the strength to walk it.

Kairos turned away and began preparing the fire, his movements quiet and methodical. Elera sat down beside him, the moonstone still clutched in her hand, its soft glow reflecting in the flickering firelight.

As the fire crackled and the night deepened, Elera found herself thinking about her brother, Seren. She hadn't told him about the journey she was on, about the magic she had witnessed or the moon's call that had brought her here. He wouldn't have understood, and yet she felt a pang of guilt for leaving him behind.

Will the moonstone lead me back to him? she wondered. *Or will it lead me somewhere I've never been before?*

As if sensing her thoughts, the moonstone pulsed gently in her hand, its light growing slightly brighter before fading again. Elera took a deep breath, reminding herself of Runa's words: *The moon's light is a reflection of what is within you. Let it guide you, and you will find the answers you seek.*

The moonstone's glow was steady now, its presence a quiet reassurance. Whatever lay ahead, Elera knew that the moon was watching over her. And as long as she followed its light—whether in the form of the moon above or the stone in her hand—she would find her way.

Chapter 9: The Silent Village

The next morning, the pale light of dawn filtered into the cave, casting soft shadows on the walls as Elera and Kairos prepared to continue their journey. The fire had long since burned out, and the air inside the cave was cool and still. Elera held the moonstone tightly in her hand, feeling its steady pulse of energy as she tucked it safely into her pouch. Its presence was comforting, a reminder that the moon's magic was with her.

"We'll reach the base of the Hidden Peaks by nightfall if we keep moving," Kairos said, glancing up at the towering mountains in the distance. "But there's something we need to pass through first."

"What is it?" Elera asked, adjusting her cloak as they stepped out of the cave and back onto the rugged mountain path.

Kairos hesitated, his expression shadowed. "A village. It lies at the base of the peaks, and we'll need to pass through it to continue our journey. But..." He trailed off, his eyes narrowing slightly. "The village is not like any other."

Elera frowned. "What do you mean?"

"The village is under a curse," Kairos said quietly. "A long time ago, something happened there—something tied to the moon's magic. Now, no one in the village speaks. They live in silence, and no one knows why."

A shiver ran down Elera's spine. A village cursed into silence? The idea seemed impossible, but then again, after everything she had already seen on this journey—the moon's song, the Silver River, the spirits in the Moonlit Grove—nothing seemed impossible anymore.

"Is it dangerous?" Elera asked, her voice cautious.

Kairos shook his head. "Not in the way you'd expect. The people there mean no harm, but the silence... it can be unsettling. And there's more to the curse than just silence. Something lingers there—something connected to the moon."

Elera felt a knot form in her stomach. She had faced shadows and enchanted rivers, but the thought of entering a village filled with people who couldn't speak made her uneasy. Still, she knew they had no choice. The Hidden Peaks were waiting, and this village was the only way through.

They walked in silence for most of the morning, the rugged terrain growing steeper as they descended from the mountain pass and approached the valley where the village lay. The landscape was stark and barren, the trees sparse and twisted, their branches reaching toward the sky like skeletal hands.

By midday, they reached the outskirts of the village. Elera's heart pounded in her chest as they crossed a small wooden bridge over a dry riverbed and entered the village proper. It was eerily quiet. No birds sang, no wind rustled the leaves, and the usual sounds of daily life—voices, laughter, the clatter of tools—were absent.

The village itself looked ordinary enough: small cottages with thatched roofs lined the narrow dirt streets, and gardens grew in neat rows behind the houses. Smoke curled from a few chimneys, indicating that the villagers were home. Yet there was an unnatural stillness to the place, as though time had stopped.

Elera's steps slowed as they entered the center of the village, her eyes scanning the area for any sign of life. She spotted a few people—an old man sitting on a bench, a woman hanging laundry, a child playing with a small wooden toy—but none of them spoke. They moved in silence, their faces blank and expressionless, as if they were unaware of the world around them.

"It's real," Elera whispered, her voice barely audible. "The curse."

Kairos nodded grimly. "It's real."

Elera's gaze was drawn to a tall building in the center of the village—a church, its steeple rising high above the rooftops. The door was slightly ajar, and a faint, eerie light flickered inside. Something about the church pulled at her, as if it held the key to the village's curse.

"Do you think the answer is in there?" Elera asked, nodding toward the church.

Kairos followed her gaze and frowned. "It might be. The moon's magic is strong in this village. Whatever happened here, it's connected to the moon, just like everything else we've encountered."

Elera took a deep breath and stepped toward the church, her heart pounding in her chest. As they approached the entrance, the heavy wooden door creaked open, revealing a dimly lit interior. The air inside was thick with dust, and the faint smell of old wood and incense lingered in the air.

The church was empty, save for a few rows of wooden pews and a stone altar at the far end. The flickering light that Elera had seen from outside came from a single candle burning on the altar, its flame small and weak. Above the altar, a large stained-glass window depicted the full moon, its silvery light streaming down on a scene of villagers gathered in worship.

Elera frowned, studying the window. Something about it felt wrong. The villagers in the stained glass were smiling, their faces full of life, but the moon above them seemed different—darker, more sinister. Its light wasn't the soft, comforting glow she had come to know. It was harsh, almost malevolent.

"There's something wrong with this place," Elera whispered, stepping closer to the altar. "The moon... it's different."

Kairos moved to stand beside her, his eyes narrowing as he studied the window. "This isn't the moon we've been following," he murmured. "This is a twisted reflection of it. The villagers must have been trying to harness the moon's magic, but something went wrong. The curse came from this."

Elera's skin prickled with unease. "What do we do?"

Kairos didn't answer right away. He stepped forward, his hand resting on the stone altar, his expression thoughtful. "The silence in this village... it's more than just a curse. The people here tried to control the moon's power, but instead, they were cut off from it. The silence is a punishment for their pride."

Elera's stomach tightened. "But why can't they speak? What does that have to do with the moon?"

Kairos turned to her, his face grim. "The moon's magic is tied to love and trust, remember? The villagers wanted to use that magic for their own gain, to control it. But in doing so, they broke the very bond that gives the moon its power—the bond of connection, the power of communication and understanding. The silence is a reflection of that broken bond."

Elera's heart ached for the villagers, trapped in a world where they could no longer speak, no longer connect with one another. It was a punishment worse than any physical pain—a silence that cut deeper than words could express.

"There has to be a way to break the curse," Elera said, her voice filled with determination. "We have to help them."

Kairos nodded slowly. "There might be. But it won't be easy."

Just then, the moonstone in Elera's pouch began to pulse, its soft light growing brighter and brighter. She gasped, pulling it out and holding it in her palm. The moonstone glowed with an intensity she hadn't seen before, as if it was reacting to the village's curse, sensing the need for its power.

"The moonstone," Elera breathed. "It's trying to show us something."

Kairos' eyes widened. "It must be the key. The moonstone holds the magic of trust and connection—everything the villagers lost. If we use it here, it might be able to restore what was broken."

Elera's pulse quickened as she stepped forward, the moonstone glowing brightly in her hand. She approached the altar, feeling the weight of the villagers' silence pressing down on her. With a deep breath, she held the moonstone above the altar, letting its light shine over the church.

For a moment, nothing happened.

Then, slowly, a soft hum filled the air—the same melodic hum Elera had heard in the Moonlit Grove, the song of the moon. The sound grew louder, echoing through the empty church, and as it did, the stained-glass window above the altar began to glow with a soft, silvery light.

The light spread throughout the church, filling every corner, every shadow, until the entire building was bathed in the moon's gentle glow. Elera felt a warmth in her chest, a connection forming between her, the moonstone, and the village itself.

Outside, the silence broke.

Voices—soft at first, then growing louder—filled the air. Elera rushed to the door, her heart racing as she stepped outside and saw the villagers standing in the streets, their faces filled with wonder and confusion. They were speaking, laughing, crying—finally free from the curse that had held them captive for so long.

Chapter 10: Whispers of the Night Wind

As they left the now-silent village behind, the distant peaks of the Hidden Mountains loomed larger against the sky, stark and foreboding. The moon, though not yet full, was a pale crescent high in the sky, offering a sliver of light as Elera and Kairos continued their journey. The atmosphere had shifted since they broke the curse in the village, and while the air was lighter without the weight of the curse's silence, Elera couldn't shake the feeling that something darker awaited them in the mountains ahead.

Kairos remained quiet, his usual serious expression more intense than before. His eyes were fixed on the peaks, his mind clearly focused on whatever trials lay ahead. Elera glanced at him, sensing that he had been growing more distant as they neared their goal. She had come to trust Kairos implicitly, but she still knew so little about him. He carried secrets—dark ones, she suspected—and soon, she knew they would need to confront whatever burdens he was holding.

As dusk settled over the land, the wind began to pick up, gusting through the trees and across the rocky terrain. It wasn't an ordinary wind. This wind had a voice. It carried whispers, soft and low, like the rustling of leaves but with a rhythm and tone that sounded almost like words. Elera slowed her steps, tilting her head to listen.

"Do you hear that?" she asked, her voice barely above a whisper.

Kairos stopped and turned toward her, his face grim. "Yes. It's the Night Wind."

"The Night Wind?" Elera echoed, feeling a shiver run down her spine. She had never heard of such a thing before, but the way Kairos said it made it sound like a danger they should avoid.

"It only blows in these mountains," Kairos explained. "It's said to be a remnant of ancient magic—voices of those who once tried to control the moon's power but failed. Their whispers are carried on the wind, warning those who walk these paths. But the wind doesn't just warn; it also tests."

"Tests?" Elera asked, her heart tightening with unease.

Kairos nodded. "It speaks to your fears. It tries to lead you astray. If you listen too closely, the Night Wind can pull you off the path and into the shadows."

Elera swallowed hard. The thought of a wind that whispered to her fears, that tried to lead her astray, was terrifying. She had faced shadows and curses, but this felt more personal—something that could creep into her mind and twist her thoughts.

"How do we stop it?" Elera asked, trying to keep the fear out of her voice.

"We can't stop it," Kairos replied. "But we can resist it. Stay focused on the path, on the light of the moon. Don't let the wind distract you."

Elera nodded, determined to stay strong, but as they continued walking, the whispers grew louder. They weren't just random sounds anymore. They were words—clear and deliberate, calling out to her from the dark corners of her mind.

"Elera..."

She froze, her heart skipping a beat. The voice was soft, almost comforting, but it wasn't Kairos. It was familiar, though—too familiar.

"Elera..." the voice whispered again, this time louder. "You don't belong here..."

She spun around, looking behind her, but there was no one there. Just the wind, swirling around the trees and rocks, whispering in her ears.

"Do you hear it?" she asked, her voice trembling.

Kairos didn't stop walking, but his expression grew even more serious. "Don't listen to it. It's not real. The wind takes the voices of those you trust most and twists them."

Elera clenched her fists, trying to block out the sound, but the voice grew stronger, more insistent.

"You should go back, Elera. You're not ready for this..."

It was Seren's voice. Her brother's voice, clear as day, speaking through the wind. But she knew it couldn't be him. He was far away, back in the village, unaware of the dangers she was facing here.

"You're too weak, Elera. You'll never make it. Turn back before it's too late..."

Elera's breath quickened. The words hit her harder than she expected. Her brother had never said those things to her, had never doubted her, but hearing his voice in this way—it made her doubt herself.

She slowed her pace, glancing up at the peaks in the distance. The path ahead seemed endless, treacherous, and cold. Could she really make it? Was she strong enough to face whatever the Hidden Peaks held?

Kairos noticed her hesitation and turned to face her, his voice cutting through the wind. "Elera, don't listen to it. The wind preys on your doubts. It's not your brother's voice. It's only trying to stop you."

Elera nodded, trying to shake off the fear that had settled over her. But the whispers didn't stop. They grew louder, more insistent, filling her mind with doubts and fears she hadn't even realized she had.

"You're all alone out here, Elera. No one can save you... not even Kairos..."

Her eyes widened, and she looked at Kairos, who was watching her carefully. Could he hear the whispers too? Were they saying the same things to him?

The wind howled, and for a brief moment, Elera thought she saw a shadowy figure standing at the edge of the path, just out of sight. It was a tall figure, cloaked in darkness, its face hidden. The figure raised its hand, beckoning her toward it.

"Come closer, Elera... you don't have to be afraid..."

Elera blinked, and the figure was gone. She gasped, her heart pounding. Was it real? Or was it another trick of the wind?

Kairos stepped closer to her, his voice calm but firm. "Elera, look at me. Focus."

She met his gaze, and the intensity in his eyes steadied her. The whispers were still there, but Kairos' voice cut through them like a blade of light.

"We're almost there," he said, his hand resting on her shoulder. "The wind will get stronger the closer we get to the peaks, but we're not alone. The moon's light is with us."

Elera nodded, her breathing steadying. She glanced up at the sky, where the crescent moon hung above them, its light faint but constant. The moonstone in her pouch pulsed gently, as if reminding her that it, too, was there, watching over them.

With renewed determination, she continued walking, her steps more deliberate now. The whispers still echoed in her ears, but she refused to listen. The wind was strong, but the moon's magic was stronger. She had to trust that.

As they climbed higher, the path grew steeper and more difficult. The wind howled through the narrow mountain pass, carrying with it more voices—voices of doubt, fear, and despair. But Elera kept her gaze fixed on the path ahead, her heart focused on the moon's light.

Kairos led the way, his presence steady and unwavering. Elera didn't know what the wind was whispering to him, but she sensed that he, too, was battling his own fears. Yet he didn't falter. His determination was unshakable, and Elera drew strength from that.

After what felt like hours, the wind began to die down. The whispers grew fainter, and the air became still. They had passed through the worst of it.

Elera let out a shaky breath, her legs trembling from the effort of climbing and resisting the wind's pull. She looked around, realizing they had reached a plateau. Below them, the village was a distant speck, and above them, the Hidden Peaks rose sharply against the night sky.

Chapter 11: Kairos' Revelation

Elera's legs ached from the climb, but she pushed herself to keep moving. Each step brought them closer to the heart of the moon's magic, the place where all their questions would be answered.

But as they climbed higher, Elera couldn't help but notice the tension in Kairos. He moved with his usual quiet grace, but there was something different about him now—something darker. His expression had grown more guarded, his eyes distant. Elera had always known that Kairos carried secrets, but now those secrets seemed to weigh more heavily on him than ever before.

"Kairos," Elera said softly as they paused to rest on a narrow ledge, the wind tugging at their cloaks. "What's wrong? You've been... different since we entered the mountains."

Kairos didn't answer right away. He stood at the edge of the ledge, staring out at the peaks rising in the distance, his face unreadable. The silence stretched on, the only sound the howling wind and the distant call of an eagle soaring overhead.

Finally, after what felt like an eternity, Kairos spoke. "There's something you need to know, Elera. Something I haven't told you."

Elera's heart skipped a beat. She had known this moment would come eventually—the moment when Kairos would reveal whatever burden he had been carrying since they first met. But now that it was here, she wasn't sure if she was ready to hear it.

"What is it?" she asked quietly, her voice filled with both curiosity and apprehension.

Kairos took a deep breath, his gaze still fixed on the distant peaks. "The moon's magic... it's not just a force that guides us. It's a power that binds us all together, connecting everything under its light. But that power—like all magic—can be dangerous if it's misused."

Elera nodded slowly, listening intently. She had already seen the dangers of the moon's magic—the curse of the silent village, the treacherous winds that whispered lies—but she had always felt that the moon's light was ultimately a force for good. It was something pure, something beautiful.

But Kairos' tone suggested otherwise.

"There's a reason I know so much about the moon's magic," Kairos continued, his voice low. "A reason I've been able to guide you through all of this."

Elera frowned. "What do you mean?"

Kairos turned to face her, and for the first time, Elera saw a flicker of vulnerability in his dark eyes. It was as if the mask he had been wearing—the mask of calm, quiet strength—had finally cracked.

"I come from a family that was once tasked with protecting the moon's secrets," Kairos said, his voice barely above a whisper. "For generations, we were the keepers of the moonstone, entrusted with ensuring that its magic was never used for the wrong purposes. But... we failed."

Elera's breath caught in her throat. "Failed? How?"

Kairos clenched his fists, his jaw tightening as he spoke. "Years ago, my family was betrayed. Someone—someone we trusted—stole the moonstone and tried to use its power for themselves. They believed they could control the moon's magic, bend it to their will. But they were wrong. The moon's magic isn't something that can be controlled. It's something that must be respected, understood."

"What happened?" Elera asked, her voice barely a whisper.

Kairos' eyes darkened. "The moonstone shattered. The magic it contained was released, wild and unchecked. My family was torn apart. Some died, others were lost. And I... I was left to pick up the pieces."

Elera felt a wave of sadness wash over her as she looked at Kairos, understanding now why he had always seemed so distant, so burdened. He had been carrying the weight of this tragedy for years, the responsibility of his family's failure pressing down on him like a heavy stone.

"I'm so sorry, Kairos," Elera said softly, reaching out to touch his arm. "You've been through so much."

Kairos shook his head, his expression hardening. "It's not just my past, Elera. It's my present. The reason I've been guiding you on this journey isn't just because I know the way. It's because I need to fix what my family broke. I need to restore the moonstone's power and make sure it's protected."

Elera's heart raced as she realized what Kairos was saying. "You mean... the moonstone I carry?"

Kairos nodded, his gaze intense. "The moonstone you found is the last fragment of what was once whole. It's a piece of the power my family lost. And I believe that when we reach the heart of the Hidden Peaks, we can restore it—bring the moon's magic back into balance."

Elera stared at him, her mind racing. She had known from the moment she found the moonstone that it was important, but she hadn't realized just how deeply connected it was to Kairos' past—or how critical it was to the future of the moon's magic.

"But why didn't you tell me this before?" Elera asked, her voice tinged with hurt. "Why keep it a secret?"

Kairos looked away, his expression pained. "Because I wasn't sure if I could trust myself. The last time my family tried to control the moon's magic, it ended in disaster. I didn't want to repeat their mistakes."

Elera felt a pang of empathy for him. Kairos had been carrying the weight of his family's failure for so long, trying to atone for something that wasn't entirely his fault. And now, he was faced with the task of restoring the very power that had caused so much pain.

"You're not alone in this," Elera said firmly, stepping closer to him. "We'll restore the moonstone together. We'll make sure the magic is protected."

Kairos' eyes softened, and for the first time, Elera saw a flicker of hope in his gaze. "Thank you, Elera. I've carried this burden alone for so long, I didn't know if I could trust anyone else with it."

Elera smiled gently. "You don't have to do it alone anymore."

Kairos gave her a small, grateful nod. "We're close to the heart of the Hidden Peaks now. That's where the moonstone must be restored. But there's one more thing you need to know."

Elera raised an eyebrow. "What is it?"

Kairos hesitated, his expression darkening once more. "When the moonstone shattered, it released not just magic, but something darker—something that has been waiting in the shadows ever since. If we're going to restore the moonstone, we'll have to face it."

Elera's pulse quickened. "What kind of darkness?"

"A shadow," Kairos said quietly. "A reflection of the moon's light, twisted by greed and betrayal. It's been waiting for us—for someone to try to restore the moonstone. And when we reach the heart of the peaks, it will come for us."

Elera felt a chill run down her spine. The journey had been filled with dangers, but the idea of facing a shadow twisted by the moon's magic was more terrifying than anything she had imagined.

"But we can stop it, right?" she asked, trying to keep the fear out of her voice.

Kairos met her gaze, his eyes filled with determination. "We can. But only if we trust the moon's light—and each other."

Chapter 12: The Dance of the Full Moon

The sun had set by the time Elera and Kairos reached the base of the final ascent into the Hidden Peaks. The sky above them had darkened, and the crescent moon from earlier in the journey was now a full, glowing orb, hanging heavy and bright above the mountains. Its light bathed the peaks in silver, illuminating the jagged rocks and casting long shadows that seemed to shift and move with a life of their own.

As they stood at the foot of the climb, Elera's heart pounded in her chest. She could feel the moonstone in her pouch pulsing with energy, growing warmer as they neared the heart of the peaks. The air around them felt charged, humming with magic—both light and dark.

"This is it," Kairos said quietly, his voice barely audible over the soft wind that blew through the narrow mountain pass. "The heart of the moon's power lies at the summit. And so does the shadow."

Elera nodded, her breath catching in her throat. She had known this moment was coming, the final confrontation with the darkness that had been waiting for them. But now that they were here, so close to the source of the moon's magic, she couldn't help but feel a mix of fear and awe.

"How do we stop the shadow?" Elera asked, glancing up at the towering peaks above. "What if it's too strong?"

Kairos shook his head, his expression somber. "The shadow is a reflection of the moon's light, twisted by the greed and betrayal that shattered the moonstone. But light and shadow cannot exist without each other. To defeat it, we have to embrace the full power of the moonstone, restore the balance between the light and the darkness."

Elera swallowed hard, her mind racing. She wasn't sure how they were supposed to "embrace" the shadow, especially when it had the potential to consume them. But she trusted Kairos, and more importantly, she trusted the moon's magic. The moonstone had guided them this far, and she believed that it would continue to protect them—if they could stay true to its light.

They began the final climb, scaling the narrow path that led up the mountainside. The terrain was rough, and the air grew colder the higher they climbed, but the light of the full moon illuminated their way, casting a silvery glow on the rocks beneath their feet.

The ascent was steep and treacherous, with loose stones slipping beneath their boots and sheer cliffs dropping away on either side. Elera's muscles ached with the effort, but she pushed herself forward, her mind focused on the moonstone and the task ahead.

As they neared the summit, the path leveled out into a wide, flat plateau. The view from the top was breathtaking—the full moon hung low in the sky, its light reflecting off the snow-capped peaks that stretched out in every direction. But there was something else, too.

In the center of the plateau stood a massive, stone circle, ancient and weathered by time. The stones were arranged in a perfect ring, and in the center of the circle was a smooth, flat slab of rock. It looked like an altar—an altar dedicated to the moon.

"This is where it will happen," Kairos said quietly, stepping forward toward the stone circle. "This is where we'll restore the moonstone."

Elera followed him, her heart racing as they approached the altar. The air inside the circle was thick with magic—she could feel it vibrating through the ground beneath her feet, humming through the stones. And as they stepped inside the ring, the moonstone in her pouch began to glow more brightly, its light almost blinding.

Kairos turned to face her, his expression grave. "Are you ready?"

Elera took a deep breath and nodded, though her hands trembled as she pulled the moonstone from her pouch. Its surface pulsed with a bright, silvery light, glowing with a power that felt almost too strong to contain. She could feel its energy coursing through her, filling her with both fear and determination.

Together, they stepped toward the altar.

Kairos reached out and placed his hands on the smooth stone surface, his eyes closing as he focused on the task ahead. Elera stood beside him, holding the moonstone in her hands, its light spilling over the stone like liquid silver.

For a moment, everything was still.

Then, without warning, the ground beneath them began to tremble. Elera gasped, stumbling back as the stones around the altar began to glow with the same silvery light as the moonstone. The wind picked up, swirling around them in a vortex of energy, and above them, the moon seemed to grow brighter, its light intensifying until the entire plateau was bathed in an otherworldly glow.

But the light wasn't alone.

From the shadows at the edge of the circle, something dark and formless began to emerge. It was like a living shadow, writhing and twisting as it moved, its shape constantly shifting. The air around it seemed to warp, and as it drew closer, Elera felt a cold, suffocating dread wash over her.

The shadow.

"It's here," Kairos said, his voice tense. "Get ready."

Elera's heart raced as the shadow moved toward them, its presence heavy and oppressive. She could feel its darkness pressing in on her, threatening to pull her under, to consume her completely. But the moonstone's light flared brighter in her hands, pushing back against the darkness.

The shadow stopped at the edge of the circle, as if testing the boundaries of the moon's magic. Then, slowly, it began to change. The dark, shifting mass condensed, taking on a more solid form. And as it did, Elera's breath caught in her throat.

The shadow had taken the shape of a figure—a tall, cloaked figure with hollow, glowing eyes. It stood just outside the circle, its gaze fixed on them, its presence both terrifying and mesmerizing.

"This is what's left of the one who tried to control the moon's magic," Kairos said, his voice tight. "The shadow of their greed, their betrayal. It's been waiting here, waiting for someone to try to restore the moonstone."

Elera's hands trembled as she clutched the moonstone tighter, its light pulsing in rhythm with her racing heart. The shadow figure stepped closer, its movements slow and deliberate, like a predator stalking its prey.

"We can't let it stop us," Kairos said, stepping closer to Elera. "The moonstone's light is the only thing keeping it at bay. We have to restore the balance now, before it grows stronger."

Elera nodded, though fear clawed at her insides. She could feel the shadow's pull, its darkness tugging at the edges of her mind, trying to fill her with doubt, with despair. But she fought against it, focusing on the moonstone's light, letting its energy flow through her.

"Kairos," she whispered, her voice shaking. "What if we fail?"

"We won't," he said firmly, his eyes locked on hers. "We've come too far to fail now."

Elera swallowed hard, her gaze flicking back to the shadow figure. It was so close now, its hollow eyes glowing with malice, its form dark and twisted. The moonstone's light flared again, and for a moment, the shadow recoiled, hissing as if in pain.

But it didn't retreat.

With a deep breath, Elera stepped forward, raising the moonstone high above her head. The light from the stone blazed brighter than ever, filling the entire plateau with its glow.

"We restore the moonstone now," Elera said, her voice steady despite the fear that threatened to overwhelm her. "For the moon. For the balance."

Kairos nodded, placing his hands on the altar once more. Together, they focused their energy, their will, on the moonstone. Elera felt the power of the moon flowing through her, through Kairos, through the very stones of the mountain itself.

The shadow figure hissed again, its form flickering as the light grew brighter. But it didn't retreat. It lunged.

In that moment, Elera understood what she had to do. The shadow wasn't just something to be fought—it was something that had to be faced, accepted. The moon's light and the darkness it cast were two sides of the same magic, and to restore the balance, she had to embrace both.

With a steady hand, Elera lowered the moonstone to the altar, its light bathing the entire stone circle in a radiant glow. She closed her eyes, allowing the moon's magic to flow through her, and whispered a quiet prayer to the moon itself.

The light flared one last time, brighter than the sun, and then...

Silence.

When Elera opened her eyes, the shadow was gone.

The moonstone lay on the altar, whole and glowing with a soft, steady light. The balance had been restored.

Chapter 13: A Shadow in the Light

Kairos stared at the moonstone, his expression unreadable. He had been quiet ever since the shadow disappeared, his eyes fixed on the glowing stone as if he were waiting for something. Elera watched him, unsure of what to say. The journey had led them here, to the heart of the moon's magic, and they had succeeded in restoring the moonstone's power. But there was a heaviness in the air, a weight that hadn't lifted with the victory.

"Kairos," Elera said softly, stepping closer to him. "What's wrong?"

Kairos didn't answer right away. He continued to stare at the moonstone, his jaw clenched, his dark eyes shadowed with something Elera couldn't quite understand.

"Kairos," she repeated, gently touching his arm. "We did it. The moonstone is restored. The shadow is gone."

Kairos finally tore his gaze away from the stone and looked at her. His eyes were filled with a strange mix of relief and sorrow, and when he spoke, his voice was quiet, almost distant. "Yes, we restored the moonstone. But the shadow isn't truly gone."

Elera's heart skipped a beat. "What do you mean? It disappeared."

Kairos shook his head, his expression grim. "The shadow was only a reflection of the darkness that lingers in the moon's magic. It can't be destroyed completely—it's part of the balance. Light and shadow, magic and darkness—they exist together. The shadow will always be there, just as the light will."

Elera frowned, trying to process what he was saying. "But we defeated it. We stopped it from consuming the moonstone."

Kairos nodded, but his eyes were still troubled. "We stopped it this time. But the shadow is drawn to the moon's magic. As long as the moonstone exists, the shadow will continue to return. It's a cycle—one that can't be broken."

A chill ran down Elera's spine. She had thought that restoring the moonstone would be the end of their journey, that the darkness had been vanquished. But now, hearing Kairos' words, she realized that their victory wasn't as complete as she had hoped.

"Then what was the point of all of this?" Elera asked, her voice tinged with frustration. "If the shadow is going to come back, if the darkness can't be destroyed, then what did we accomplish?"

Kairos turned away, his shoulders tense. "We restored the balance. That's all we can do. The moon's magic is too powerful to control completely. Our task was to keep it in balance, to ensure that the light and the shadow coexist."

Elera's heart sank. She had wanted to believe that their journey would bring an end to the danger, that they had saved the moon's magic once and for all. But now, it seemed that the darkness would always be there, waiting to rise again.

For a long moment, neither of them spoke. The wind whispered through the mountains, and the moonstone continued to pulse with its gentle light, a quiet reminder of the power they had fought to protect.

Finally, Elera broke the silence. "There's something you're not telling me, isn't there?"

Kairos stiffened but didn't respond.

"Kairos," she said, her voice soft but insistent. "You've carried this burden alone for so long. You don't have to anymore. Whatever it is, you can tell me."

Kairos closed his eyes, his hands clenching into fists at his sides. For a moment, Elera thought he wouldn't answer. But then, with a deep, shuddering breath, he spoke.

"The shadow isn't just a reflection of the moon's magic," he said quietly. "It's a reflection of me."

Elera's breath caught in her throat. "What do you mean?"

Kairos turned to face her, his expression filled with pain. "When the moonstone shattered all those years ago, it wasn't just the moon's magic that was broken. Part of that darkness—the shadow—it was drawn to me. It's been inside me ever since."

Elera stared at him, her heart racing. "You... you're connected to the shadow?"

Kairos nodded, his eyes filled with anguish. "I've felt it ever since that day. The darkness inside me. It's why I've been able to sense the moon's magic, why I knew how to guide you. But it's also why I've always kept my distance, why I couldn't let you get too close. The shadow is a part of me, and I don't know if it can ever be separated."

Elera's mind raced, trying to make sense of what he was telling her. Kairos had always been distant, always seemed to carry a weight that he refused to share. But now, she understood why. He had been living with this darkness inside him, this connection to the very shadow they had fought to defeat.

"Kairos," she whispered, stepping closer to him. "This isn't your fault. You didn't choose this."

Kairos shook his head, his voice filled with bitterness. "No, but I've lived with it. I've felt the shadow growing stronger inside me, and I've fought to keep it at bay. But I'm afraid that one day... I won't be able to."

Elera reached out, placing her hand on his arm. "You've already proven that you're stronger than the shadow. You helped restore the moonstone. You fought against the darkness and won."

Kairos looked at her, his eyes filled with doubt. "For now. But the shadow will always be there, waiting for a moment of weakness."

Elera felt a surge of emotion—compassion, fear, and something else she couldn't quite name. She had come to care for Kairos deeply, and the thought of him battling this darkness alone broke her heart. But she refused to believe that the shadow would win.

"You're not alone in this," Elera said firmly, her hand tightening on his arm. "I'm here with you, and I'm not going to let the shadow take you."

Kairos looked at her, his eyes searching her face as if he couldn't quite believe what he was hearing. "Elera... you don't understand. This darkness, it's inside me. I don't know if I can ever be free of it."

"You don't have to be free of it," Elera said softly, her voice filled with conviction. "The moon's magic is about balance, remember? Light and shadow. You've been trying to fight the darkness on your own, but you don't have to. You can face it with me. We can keep it in balance together."

Kairos stared at her, his expression conflicted. But slowly, the tension in his shoulders eased, and a flicker of hope appeared in his eyes.

"You really believe that?" he asked, his voice barely above a whisper.

Elera smiled, her heart filled with certainty. "I do. You've carried this burden for long enough. Let me help you."

For a long moment, Kairos said nothing. Then, finally, he nodded, his gaze softening. "Thank you, Elera. I've been alone for so long, I didn't know how to let anyone in. But... I want to try."

Elera's smile widened, and she felt a surge of warmth in her chest. "We'll figure it out together."

Chapter 14: The Cradle of Stars

The descent from the Hidden Peaks felt lighter, though no less significant, than the climb had been. Elera and Kairos had faced the moon's shadow and emerged with a renewed sense of purpose, their bond strengthened by the trials they had overcome. The air was crisp, and the moonstone, now whole and pulsing softly, glowed faintly in Elera's pouch as they walked.

It wasn't long before the terrain began to change once again. The rocky paths gave way to softer ground, and soon they found themselves entering a vast, open valley. The sky overhead seemed impossibly large, a dome of deep indigo sprinkled with stars that twinkled like tiny diamonds. There was something ethereal about this place, something otherworldly.

"This is the Cradle of Stars," Kairos said quietly, his voice full of reverence. "One of the oldest places tied to the moon's magic. It's said that the first keepers of the moonstone came from here, long before my family took up the mantle."

Elera glanced around in awe. The valley stretched out before them like a sea of grass, with small mounds of earth rising and falling like gentle waves. In the distance, she could see clusters of stones, arranged in patterns that seemed too deliberate to be natural. And above it all, the stars glittered like distant fires, their light bathing the landscape in a silvery glow.

"I've heard stories about this place," Elera said softly. "The elders in my village used to talk about it like it was a dream—something too ancient and far away to be real."

"It's real," Kairos said, his gaze fixed on the sky. "And it's more than just a place. The magic here is old, deeper than anything we've seen so far."

Elera felt a shiver of excitement run down her spine. She had thought their journey was nearing its end after restoring the moonstone, but now it seemed that the Cradle of Stars held even more secrets. And perhaps, more answers.

As they walked further into the valley, the ground beneath their feet seemed to shimmer, as if the very earth was alive with the magic of the stars above. The air was cool, but not cold, and the wind carried a faint, melodic hum—a sound that reminded Elera of the moon's song she had heard before.

"Why did we come here?" Elera asked, her voice soft as she stared up at the sky. "What does this place have to do with the moonstone?"

Kairos hesitated, his eyes scanning the horizon. "The moonstone was restored, but it's still connected to everything—the moon, the stars, the magic that runs through the earth. The Cradle of Stars is the final piece of the puzzle. There's something here we need to see. Something the moon wants to show us."

Elera frowned, her curiosity piqued. She had felt the pull of the moon's magic guiding her throughout their journey, but now it was different. The air here was charged with an ancient power, a power that seemed to be waiting for them.

They walked in silence for a while, the grass soft beneath their feet and the stars growing brighter with each passing moment. The valley seemed to stretch on forever, but eventually, they came to a clearing—a wide, open space surrounded by the ancient stone circles Elera had seen from a distance.

In the center of the clearing was a pool of water, perfectly still and reflecting the stars above like a mirror. The sight of it took Elera's breath away. It was as though the sky itself had been captured in the pool, its reflection so clear that it felt like she could reach down and touch the stars.

"This is the heart of the Cradle," Kairos said, stepping closer to the edge of the pool. "The water here is said to hold the light of the stars, just as the moonstone holds the light of the moon. It's a place of reflection."

Elera knelt beside the pool, staring into its depths. The stars shimmered in the water, but there was something more—something beneath the surface. She leaned in closer, her eyes narrowing as she tried to make out what it was.

And then she saw it.

In the depths of the pool, beneath the stars' reflection, there was an image—a vision, faint but growing clearer the longer she looked. It was a scene from the past, like a memory suspended in time. Elera gasped as she realized what she was seeing.

The image showed a group of people, dressed in robes of silver and blue, standing in a circle around a glowing stone—another moonstone. Their faces were serene, their hands raised toward the sky as if in prayer. But there was something else—something dark. A shadow lingered at the edges of the vision, twisting and writhing as it crept closer to the group.

"That's the first moonstone," Kairos said softly, his voice full of awe. "The first keepers of the moon's magic. This is where it all began."

Elera's heart raced as she watched the vision unfold. The group of keepers continued their ritual, unaware of the shadow that was creeping closer. And then, in a sudden burst of movement, the shadow lunged forward, engulfing the moonstone in its darkness. The keepers cried out, their serene faces turning to fear as the shadow consumed the light.

The vision ended abruptly, the water returning to its still, reflective state. Elera sat back, her heart pounding in her chest.

"That's how it happened," she whispered, her voice trembling. "That's how the shadow began."

Kairos nodded, his expression grim. "The shadow wasn't just born from greed or betrayal. It was always there, lurking at the edges of the moon's magic, waiting for a moment of weakness."

Elera felt a chill run through her. The shadow was older than she had realized—older than even Kairos' family's connection to the moonstone. It had been part of the magic from the very beginning, always waiting, always watching.

"But the moonstone was restored," Elera said, her voice stronger now. "We restored the balance."

Kairos looked at her, his eyes filled with determination. "We did. But the balance is delicate. The shadow will always be part of the moon's magic, just as the light is. What we saw in the pool was a reminder—of how easily the balance can be broken, how quickly the darkness can take over."

Elera nodded, her mind racing. She had known from the start that their journey was about more than just restoring the moonstone—it was about understanding the deeper forces at play, the light and shadow that were intertwined in the magic of the world. But seeing the vision in the pool had made it all so much clearer.

The balance they had fought to restore wasn't permanent. It was something that needed to be protected, nurtured. The shadow would always be there, waiting for a moment of weakness. And it was up to those who understood the magic to keep the light alive.

"We can't let this happen again," Elera said, standing up and looking at Kairos with renewed resolve. "We have to protect the moonstone, protect the balance."

Kairos nodded, his gaze steady. "We will. Together."

Elera smiled, feeling a warmth spread through her chest. They had come so far, faced so many challenges, but now, standing in the Cradle of Stars, she knew that their journey had been about more than just the moonstone. It had been about understanding the responsibility that came with the magic, the power that flowed through the world and the stars above.

The Cradle of Stars was a place of reflection, of memory, but it was also a place of new beginnings. And as Elera stood beside Kairos, staring up at the endless sky, she knew that their journey wasn't over. There were still more mysteries to uncover, more magic to protect.

Chapter 15: A Rift Between Friends

Despite their shared journey, a tension had settled between them—an unspoken weight hanging over every step. Elera could feel it growing, thickening the air between them like the dark clouds that sometimes gathered over the peaks. Though they had succeeded in restoring the moonstone, the deeper truths they had uncovered in the Cradle of Stars had left scars, ones that hadn't yet healed.

Kairos walked ahead, his movements purposeful and quiet. His connection to the shadow, the darkness he carried within him, had been laid bare, but it was clear that he hadn't yet come to terms with it. Elera could sense his internal struggle, the way he carried himself with a burden that wasn't just about his past—it was about the future, too. The shadow, ever lurking at the edge of the moon's magic, wasn't something they could easily vanquish.

As the silence between them stretched on, Elera's thoughts churned. She had come to trust Kairos, to see him as a friend, but now there was something different in him, something distant. She wanted to reach out, to help him carry the weight he bore, but every time she tried, Kairos seemed to pull further away.

Finally, after what felt like hours of walking in silence, Elera couldn't hold it in any longer. She quickened her pace until she was walking beside him, matching his long strides.

"Kairos," she said softly, glancing at him, "I know you're still thinking about what we saw in the Cradle of Stars. About the shadow."

Kairos didn't meet her gaze, his eyes fixed on the path ahead. "It's not something I can just forget, Elera. The shadow is a part of me. I can't escape it, no matter how much I want to."

Elera felt a pang of frustration. She had thought they were in this together, that they had faced the shadow as a team. But Kairos' words made it clear that he still saw it as his burden alone, something he had to deal with by himself.

"You don't have to escape it," she said, trying to keep her voice steady. "We've already faced it once. We can face it again—together. You don't have to carry this alone."

Kairos stopped suddenly, turning to face her. His expression was hard, his eyes dark with something unreadable. "You don't understand, Elera. This isn't something we can just fight off and be done with. The shadow is always there, waiting. It's inside me, and one day... one day, it might be too strong for me to hold back."

Elera's heart raced. She could hear the fear in his voice, the fear of losing control, of succumbing to the darkness within him. But what stung the most was the distance he was putting between them, the way he was shutting her out.

"Kairos," she said, her voice softer now, "I've seen your strength. You've fought against the shadow before, and you won. You're not going to let it take over."

Kairos shook his head, his expression filled with frustration. "You don't get it, Elera. This isn't just about being strong enough. It's not something I can always control. And if I can't... if the shadow takes over..."

His voice trailed off, and Elera's chest tightened. She wanted to tell him that he was wrong, that they could face anything together, but a part of her knew that he was right. The shadow wasn't just an enemy they could defeat once and for all—it was something deeper, something tied to the very nature of the moon's magic. And as much as she wanted to believe that Kairos could resist it forever, the fear in his eyes told her that he wasn't so sure.

The silence between them grew heavier, the rift widening as the unspoken doubts lingered in the air.

"I just need time," Kairos said finally, his voice quiet and strained. "Time to figure out what this means for me. For us."

Elera's heart sank. She had thought that restoring the moonstone would be the end of their struggles, but now it felt like the beginning of something even more difficult. She wanted to help Kairos, to stand by him, but he was closing himself off, retreating into the darkness of his own thoughts.

"What does that mean, Kairos?" she asked, her voice trembling slightly. "Are you saying you need time away from me?"

Kairos looked at her, his expression torn. "No. That's not what I mean. I don't want to push you away, Elera, but... I don't know how to keep you safe from this."

Elera stepped closer to him, her voice firm. "I don't need you to keep me safe, Kairos. We're in this together, remember? I'm not afraid of the shadow, and I'm not afraid of you."

Kairos' eyes softened, and for a moment, Elera thought she saw a glimmer of the connection they had shared—the trust, the understanding. But then, just as quickly, his gaze darkened again.

"I'm afraid," Kairos admitted, his voice barely above a whisper. "I'm afraid of what I might become if the shadow gets stronger. And I don't want you to have to face that."

Elera's heart broke for him. She could see the conflict in his eyes, the fear of losing control and hurting the people he cared about. But she wasn't willing to let him shut her out. Not after everything they had been through together.

"You won't face it alone," she said quietly, her voice steady. "Whatever happens, I'm going to be there. You don't have to protect me from this. I'm not leaving you, Kairos. Not now, not ever."

Kairos stared at her, his expression conflicted. He wanted to believe her, she could see that, but the fear was still there, gnawing at the edges of his resolve.

"I don't deserve that," he said finally, his voice barely a whisper.

"Yes, you do," Elera said firmly, her eyes locked on his. "You've been carrying this burden alone for so long, but you don't have to anymore. Let me in, Kairos. Let me help you."

For a long moment, Kairos didn't say anything. The tension between them was thick, the unspoken fear lingering in the air like a storm cloud. But then, slowly, Kairos took a deep breath and nodded, his shoulders relaxing ever so slightly.

"Thank you, Elera," he said quietly. "I'm trying. I really am."

Elera smiled, though the rift between them still felt raw. "That's all I'm asking, Kairos. Just... don't shut me out."

Kairos gave her a small, tentative smile in return, and for the first time in hours, the air between them felt lighter. The shadows hadn't disappeared completely, but there was hope—hope that together, they could keep the balance.

They continued walking, side by side once again, but this time, there was a quiet understanding between them. The journey ahead would still be difficult, and the shadow was far from gone, but Elera knew they would face it together. She had to believe that, no matter what darkness lay ahead, their bond would be strong enough to see them through.

Chapter 16: The Mark of the Past

The rift between Elera and Kairos had not vanished completely, but a fragile understanding had emerged. Kairos had let down his guard—if only a little—and Elera had reaffirmed her promise to stand by him, no matter the shadows they faced.

Yet, as the forest grew denser and the path more rugged, Elera couldn't shake the feeling that something was following them, a presence lurking just out of sight. The trees around them were ancient, their gnarled branches intertwining above to form a canopy that blocked out much of the sky. It was peaceful, but also unsettling, as if the forest held secrets it wasn't ready to reveal.

Kairos walked ahead, his pace steady but his expression distant. He hadn't spoken much since their conversation, and while Elera was grateful for the fragile truce between them, she knew that the shadow still weighed heavily on his mind.

The morning light filtered through the trees, illuminating a clearing up ahead. As they stepped into the open space, Elera's breath caught in her throat.

The clearing was unlike anything she had ever seen. In the center stood a massive stone obelisk, its surface etched with intricate carvings that shimmered faintly in the light. The carvings depicted scenes of moonlit rituals, figures draped in flowing robes raising their hands toward the sky, and beneath them, swirling patterns of stars and shadows intertwined. The stone seemed to hum with an ancient energy, the air around it charged with magic.

"What is this place?" Elera asked, her voice hushed in awe.

Kairos stood still, staring at the obelisk with a look of quiet reverence. "This is the Mark of the Past," he said softly. "One of the oldest places tied to the moon's magic. It was here, centuries ago, that the first keepers of the moonstone swore their oath to protect the balance between light and shadow."

Elera stepped closer to the obelisk, her fingers grazing the cool surface of the stone. The carvings seemed to shift beneath her touch, the figures and symbols coming alive as if the stone were a living memory. She could feel the weight of history in this place, the echoes of those who had come before her, bound by the same promise to protect the delicate balance of the moon's magic.

"The Mark of the Past," Elera repeated, her voice barely above a whisper. "This is where it all began."

Kairos nodded, his eyes fixed on the obelisk. "This is where my ancestors took their vow. They were the first to understand the power of the moonstone, and the first to realize the danger of the shadow."

Elera glanced at him, sensing the heaviness in his voice. "You've been here before, haven't you?"

Kairos didn't answer right away. His gaze remained locked on the obelisk, his expression distant. "Once," he said finally. "A long time ago. My father brought me here when I was a boy, before everything... before the moonstone was shattered."

Elera's heart ached for him. She had known Kairos carried the weight of his family's past, but standing here, in the place where it had all begun, she could see just how deeply it affected him.

"This place holds more than just memories," Kairos continued, his voice low. "It holds the power of the oath my family swore. It's said that anyone who stands here can feel the magic of the past, the magic that binds us to the moon's light."

Elera nodded, her fingers tracing the ancient carvings. She could feel it—the energy of the place, the magic of those who had come before her. It was as if the very air was alive with the promises made here, the promises to protect the moon's magic, to keep the balance between light and shadow.

As they stood in silence, the wind stirred, rustling the leaves at the edge of the clearing. And then, without warning, the obelisk began to glow. Faint at first, but growing stronger, the carvings shimmered with a soft, silvery light that seemed to pulse in rhythm with the moonstone in Elera's pouch.

Elera gasped, stepping back in surprise. "What's happening?"

Kairos' expression darkened. "The magic here is responding to the moonstone," he said, his voice tense. "It's been dormant for centuries, waiting for the moonstone to return."

The light from the obelisk grew brighter, casting long shadows across the clearing. And then, slowly, the ground beneath them began to tremble. Elera stumbled, her heart racing as the earth shook beneath her feet. The air around them seemed to warp, the wind picking up as the magic of the obelisk surged.

"We need to get out of here," Kairos said urgently, grabbing Elera's arm. "The magic here is too strong. It's unstable."

But before they could move, the light from the obelisk flared, blinding in its intensity. Elera shielded her eyes, her heart pounding in her chest as the light swallowed the clearing. And then, just as suddenly as it had begun, the light dimmed, leaving behind a still, eerie silence.

When Elera opened her eyes, the clearing was no longer empty.

Standing in the center of the stone circle, where the obelisk had been moments before, was a figure. Tall and cloaked in shadow, its form flickered in and out of sight, as if it were not entirely part of this world. Its face was hidden beneath a dark hood, but its presence was undeniable—heavy, oppressive, and filled with a cold, malevolent energy.

Elera's breath caught in her throat. "The shadow..."

Kairos stepped forward, his hand resting on the hilt of his sword. "It's not the shadow we fought before," he said, his voice low. "This is different."

The figure stood still, its hollow eyes fixed on them, watching in silence. And then, slowly, it raised a hand, pointing directly at Kairos.

"Kairos," the figure said, its voice a low, guttural rasp that seemed to echo from the very depths of the earth. "You have returned."

Elera's heart raced. The voice was like nothing she had ever heard before—cold and ancient, filled with a power that made her skin crawl. She glanced at Kairos, whose face had gone pale, his eyes wide with shock.

"You know me?" Kairos asked, his voice trembling slightly.

The figure stepped closer, its shadowy form flickering as it moved. "I know you," it said, its voice growing louder. "I know your blood. I know your family. You carry the mark of the past, the mark of those who once swore to protect the moonstone. But you are not like them."

Kairos tensed, his hand tightening on the hilt of his sword. "What do you mean?"

The figure's voice dripped with malice. "You are tainted. The shadow has touched you. It lives inside you, festering, waiting to consume you."

Elera's breath caught in her throat. She had known Kairos was connected to the shadow, but hearing it spoken aloud like this—by something so dark, so ancient—made the reality of it even more terrifying.

Kairos took a step back, his expression hardening. "I've fought the shadow before, and I'll fight it again. You won't take me."

The figure's hollow eyes glowed faintly beneath its hood. "You cannot fight what you are," it said, its voice cold and certain. "The shadow is part of you. It has always been part of you."

Elera felt a surge of fear rise in her chest, but she pushed it down, stepping forward to stand beside Kairos. "He's not alone," she said firmly, her voice steady despite the fear gnawing at her insides. "We've already faced the shadow, and we'll face it again—together."

The figure's gaze shifted to Elera, its dark eyes narrowing. "You think you can save him?" it asked, its voice filled with contempt. "The shadow will consume him, just as it consumed those who came before. You cannot stop it."

Elera's heart pounded, but she refused to back down. "He's stronger than you think," she said, her voice filled with conviction. "And so am I."

For a moment, the figure said nothing. And then, slowly, it lowered its hand, its form flickering once more.

"We shall see," it said, its voice a low, menacing whisper. "The shadow is patient. It will wait."

And with that, the figure vanished, dissolving into the air like smoke carried away by the wind.

Elera stood frozen, her mind racing. The clearing was still once again, the only sound the soft rustle of leaves in the breeze. The obelisk had returned to its original state, its glow dimmed, as if the magic had been spent.

Kairos stood beside her, his face pale, his hands trembling. He didn't speak, but Elera could see the fear in his eyes—the fear of what the figure had said, the fear of the shadow inside him.

Elera reached out, placing a hand on his arm. "We'll face it together," she said softly. "No matter what."

Kairos nodded, though his eyes were filled with doubt. "I don't know if I can fight it, Elera," he said quietly. "I don't know if I'm strong enough."

Elera squeezed his arm gently. "You are. And you're not alone."

The silence that followed was heavy, but Elera knew that they couldn't stay here. The shadow was still out there, waiting, and they had to be ready for whatever came next.

They left the clearing, the Mark of the Past fading behind them as they continued down the path. The air was thick with uncertainty, but Elera held onto one truth: they would face the shadow together.

Chapter 17: Into the Mirrorwood

The dense forest of the Mirrorwood loomed ahead, its canopy thick and dark, casting long shadows over the narrow path. It was a forest shrouded in legend, a place that the villagers back home spoke of only in hushed tones, if at all. The Mirrorwood was said to be enchanted, filled with illusions and reflections of one's deepest fears and desires. Few who entered ever returned unchanged.

Elera's heart pounded as they crossed the threshold into the forest. The air inside the Mirrorwood was different—heavier, quieter. It was as if the very sound of their footsteps was swallowed by the trees, leaving only the faint rustling of leaves and the occasional snap of a twig underfoot.

Kairos walked beside her, his face unreadable, but Elera could sense the tension in him. The encounter at the Mark of the Past had left him shaken, and though they hadn't spoken much since, she knew the shadow's taunting words still lingered in his mind.

"This place feels wrong," Elera said quietly, glancing at the towering trees that surrounded them. The bark of the trees shimmered faintly, as if reflecting the light in ways that defied explanation.

Kairos nodded, his gaze scanning their surroundings warily. "The Mirrorwood plays tricks on the mind. It shows you what it wants you to see, what it thinks will keep you trapped."

Elera frowned. "Trapped how?"

"The forest reflects your thoughts, your fears, your desires," Kairos explained. "It can twist reality until you can't tell what's real and what's illusion. Many who enter lose themselves in the reflections, unable to find their way out."

A chill ran down Elera's spine. She had heard the stories of the Mirrorwood, of travelers who entered and were never seen again. The idea that the forest could warp reality, turning their own thoughts against them, was terrifying.

"We need to stay focused," Kairos said, his voice steady but filled with caution. "No matter what we see, we have to remember that it's not real. The Mirrorwood is just a reflection."

Elera nodded, though her heart still raced with unease. She had faced shadows, curses, and ancient magic, but this was different. The Mirrorwood wasn't an enemy she could fight—it was something far more insidious, something that would use her own mind against her.

As they ventured deeper into the forest, the path became narrower, the trees pressing in on either side. The branches above seemed to weave together like a net, blocking out much of the light. The shadows grew longer, and the air grew colder, a faint mist rising from the ground.

Elera kept her gaze forward, her hand resting on the moonstone in her pouch. Its soft pulse was a comforting reminder of the moon's magic, a light in the darkness that guided her. But even the moonstone's glow felt dimmer here, as if the forest itself was dampening its power.

The silence stretched on, broken only by the occasional creak of wood or rustle of leaves. But then, after what felt like hours, Elera began to notice something strange.

The trees ahead were no longer just trees.

At first, she thought it was a trick of the light—a shimmer at the edge of her vision. But as they walked further, the shapes among the trees became clearer. Figures moved in the shadows, their forms distorted and flickering, like reflections on the surface of a rippling pond.

Elera's breath caught in her throat. "Do you see that?"

Kairos slowed, his eyes narrowing. "Yes."

The figures were everywhere, shifting between the trees, their faces blurred and indistinct. They seemed to be watching, waiting, but they made no sound. As Elera and Kairos approached, the figures grew clearer, more defined.

And then, with a sudden jolt, Elera realized what they were.

They were reflections—of her.

Dozens of versions of herself, standing among the trees, their faces turned toward her, their eyes filled with emotions she couldn't fully comprehend. Some looked at her with fear, others with anger or sorrow. But the worst were the ones that smiled—the ones that looked at her with an eerie, unsettling calm, as if they knew something she didn't.

Elera froze, her heart pounding in her chest. "What... what is this?"

"The Mirrorwood," Kairos said quietly. "It's showing you reflections of yourself. Your fears, your doubts, your memories."

Elera's hands trembled as she looked around at the reflections. One of them stepped forward, its face contorted with anger, its eyes burning with resentment. "You think you're strong," the reflection spat, its voice harsh and accusing. "But you're weak. You've always been weak."

Elera's breath hitched. The words stung, not because they were true, but because they echoed the fears she had tried so hard to bury. The reflection was pulling from the darkest parts of her mind, from the doubts she had kept hidden, and throwing them back in her face.

Another reflection stepped forward, this one filled with sorrow, tears streaming down its face. "You left him behind," it whispered, its voice trembling with grief. "Your brother needed you, and you abandoned him."

Elera shook her head, stepping back, her heart twisting with guilt. She hadn't abandoned Seren—she had left to follow the moon's call, to protect the magic that held their world together. But the reflection's words cut deep, reminding her of the choice she had made, the people she had left behind.

The reflections pressed closer, their voices growing louder, more insistent. "You're a failure," one said. "You're not strong enough." "You'll never be what they need you to be."

Elera stumbled, her mind reeling as the voices swirled around her, each one hitting her with a new wave of doubt and fear. She wanted to scream, to tell them to stop, but the words stuck in her throat.

The Mirrorwood was doing exactly what Kairos had warned it would—twisting her thoughts, using her own mind against her.

"Elera," Kairos' voice cut through the chaos, firm and steady. "Don't listen to them. It's not real."

Elera looked at him, her chest tight with emotion. "But it feels real," she whispered, her voice trembling. "It feels like everything I've been afraid of."

Kairos stepped closer, his hand resting on her arm. "That's the Mirrorwood's power. It feeds on your fears, your insecurities. But it's not real. You're stronger than this."

Elera took a deep, shaky breath, trying to focus on Kairos' words. She closed her eyes, shutting out the reflections, the voices, the overwhelming flood of doubt. The moonstone pulsed faintly in her hand, a steady, reassuring beat.

When she opened her eyes again, the reflections had faded, their forms dissolving into the mist. The voices were gone, leaving behind only the soft rustle of leaves and the distant call of birds.

Kairos' hand remained on her arm, his touch grounding her. "You're not alone, Elera," he said softly. "You never were."

Chapter 18: The Illusion of Choice

The deeper Elera and Kairos ventured into the Mirrorwood, the more the forest seemed to close in around them. The towering trees cast long, twisting shadows, their gnarled branches creating a canopy that blocked out the sun. The air was thick, and the once comforting pulse of the moonstone in Elera's pouch felt distant, muted by the weight of the forest's magic.

Elera could sense that the Mirrorwood wasn't done with them. Its illusions had tested her once, showing her reflections of her darkest fears, but there was something more ahead—something that felt different. Stronger. The forest wasn't just a place of reflections; it was alive, its magic woven into every tree, every shadow, waiting to challenge them again.

Kairos walked beside her, his eyes scanning their surroundings, his body tense. He hadn't said much since the reflection incident, but Elera could feel the weight of his thoughts. The shadow's taunt at the Mark of the Past had shaken him, and while he had tried to push through it, the burden was still there, lingering like a dark cloud just out of reach.

"We're getting closer," Kairos said suddenly, his voice breaking the heavy silence that had settled between them. "I can feel the magic getting stronger."

Elera nodded, though her heart was pounding in her chest. She could feel it too—the pull of something powerful, something waiting for them deeper in the forest. It was as if the Mirrorwood itself was guiding them toward a place they couldn't avoid, a place where their choices would be tested.

The path ahead twisted sharply, leading them into a dense thicket where the trees grew even taller, their branches so thick that only thin beams of light managed to pierce the darkness. The shadows here felt heavier, more oppressive, and as they continued forward, Elera couldn't shake the feeling that they were being watched.

Finally, the path opened up into a small clearing. In the center stood something that made Elera's breath catch in her throat.

It was an archway, made entirely of twisted branches and vines, glowing faintly with an eerie, silvery light. The arch was ancient, the wood weathered and covered in moss, but the magic emanating from it was unmistakable.

Kairos' face grew grim. "That's not an ordinary archway," he muttered, stepping closer to examine it. "It's a portal."

"A portal?" Elera repeated, her voice filled with both curiosity and unease. "Where does it lead?"

Kairos shook his head. "I don't know. But the Mirrorwood is known for its illusions. It could take us anywhere—or show us anything."

Elera frowned, her eyes fixed on the archway. She could feel its pull, a strange, almost magnetic force drawing her toward it. But there was something else too—something darker. The archway wasn't just a portal to another place. It was a test.

"We have to go through it, don't we?" Elera asked quietly, already knowing the answer.

Kairos nodded, though his expression remained tense. "The Mirrorwood wouldn't show us this if it wasn't part of the journey. But we need to be careful. The forest's magic will use whatever's inside to challenge us—make us doubt our choices."

Elera's heart raced as she stepped toward the archway, the silvery light flickering faintly. She could feel the magic thrumming in the air, a quiet hum that seemed to vibrate through her very bones. It was a strange sensation, both comforting and terrifying, as if the forest itself was whispering to her, urging her forward.

With a deep breath, she stepped through the archway.

The world around her shifted instantly.

Elera found herself standing in a familiar place—a wide, open field, bathed in the golden light of late afternoon. The grass swayed gently in the breeze, and in the distance, she could see the silhouette of her village, Hallowvale, nestled against the horizon. Her heart skipped a beat. This was home.

But something was wrong.

The village was too still, too quiet. The familiar sounds of children playing, of carts rattling over the cobblestone streets, were absent. And there, standing at the edge of the field, was a figure she recognized all too well.

"Seren," Elera whispered, her voice trembling.

Her brother stood with his back to her, his shoulders hunched, his head bowed. He hadn't turned to face her, but Elera could feel the weight of his presence, the quiet disappointment that radiated from him.

Elera's throat tightened. She hadn't seen Seren since she left the village to follow the moon's call, to restore the moonstone and protect the balance of magic. She had told herself that her journey was necessary, that leaving Seren behind was the right choice. But now, standing here, in this illusion created by the Mirrorwood, the weight of that choice crashed down on her.

Slowly, Seren turned to face her.

His eyes were filled with sadness, his face lined with worry. "You left," he said quietly, his voice filled with hurt. "You abandoned me."

Elera's breath caught in her throat. "I didn't abandon you, Seren. I had to go. I had to protect the moon's magic."

"You always had a choice," Seren said, his voice rising slightly. "You chose to leave. You chose to leave me behind."

Tears pricked at the corners of Elera's eyes. "I didn't have a choice," she whispered, her voice trembling. "The moonstone—"

"There's always a choice," Seren interrupted, his voice hard now. "You could have stayed. You could have been here with me. But you chose to go."

Elera shook her head, the guilt and doubt swirling in her mind. She had always believed that following the moon's call was the right thing to do, that restoring the balance was worth the sacrifices. But now, standing here, facing the person she had left behind, the certainty she had clung to felt fragile.

"Seren, please," she whispered, her voice breaking. "I had to."

Seren's expression softened, but the sadness remained. "And now you're trapped in this journey, Elera. Chasing after something you may never find. What if you're wrong? What if the magic you're trying to protect is already lost?"

Elera's chest tightened. What if Seren was right? What if this journey had been in vain, and the balance they sought to restore was beyond saving?

"I'm not wrong," Elera said, though the words felt hollow. "I'm doing what I have to do."

Seren looked at her for a long moment, his eyes filled with sorrow. "I just wanted you to stay," he whispered. "I didn't want to be alone."

Elera's heart shattered at his words. She took a step toward him, but as she reached out to touch him, Seren's form flickered, dissolving into the air like smoke carried away by the wind.

Elera gasped, stumbling back as the illusion faded. The golden light of the field vanished, replaced by the dark, twisted trees of the Mirrorwood. She was back in the clearing, standing before the archway. Her chest heaved with the weight of what she had seen, of the doubts that still lingered in her heart.

Kairos stood beside her, his face pale, his expression tense. "I saw it too," he said quietly, his voice thick with emotion. "My own reflection."

Elera's heart ached for him. The Mirrorwood had shown them both what they feared most, the choices that haunted them. It had tried to break them, to make them doubt their path.

But Elera wasn't broken. Not yet.

"The forest wanted us to question our choices," Elera said softly, her voice steady despite the storm of emotions inside her. "But we have to keep going. We can't let the illusions stop us."

Chapter 19: Shadows of the Future

The further they went, the darker the forest became. The trees loomed taller, their branches interwoven in a way that blocked out even the faintest light from the moon or stars. Only the soft glow from the moonstone kept them from being swallowed by the shadows.

Kairos hadn't spoken much since they left the archway. His face was hard, his jaw set, but there was a weariness in his eyes that hadn't been there before. Whatever illusion he had faced in the Mirrorwood, it had shaken him.

Elera wanted to reach out, to reassure him as he had reassured her, but something stopped her. The journey had taken its toll on both of them, and there were some battles they each had to face alone.

As they walked, a sudden gust of wind rustled through the trees, carrying with it the faintest whisper of something familiar. Elera froze, her heart skipping a beat as the voice reached her ears.

"Elera..."

Her breath caught in her throat. She knew that voice.

"Kairos, did you hear that?" she asked, her voice trembling slightly.

Kairos stopped and turned toward her, his brow furrowed. "Hear what?"

Elera listened again, her heart pounding in her chest. The wind had died down, and the forest was once again eerily silent. But she was certain she had heard it—a voice, calling her name.

"I thought..." She shook her head, trying to clear the fear that was creeping up inside her. "Never mind. Let's keep going."

But as they continued walking, the voice came again, stronger this time.

"Elera..."

It was her brother, Seren.

Elera's pulse quickened. This wasn't like the illusions they had faced before. Seren's voice was clear, distinct. It sounded real.

"Seren?" she called out, her voice trembling. "Seren, is that you?"

Kairos stopped and turned to her, his expression alarmed. "Elera, don't. The forest is playing tricks on you."

But Elera couldn't ignore it. The voice was too real, too familiar.

"I have to find him," she said, her voice filled with urgency. "What if he's really here?"

Kairos grabbed her arm, his grip firm. "It's the Mirrorwood," he said, his voice low but intense. "It's trying to lead you astray. You know that."

Elera shook her head, pulling free from his grasp. "But what if it's not? What if he's really here? What if something's happened to him?"

Kairos opened his mouth to argue, but the look in Elera's eyes stopped him. She knew the Mirrorwood could manipulate reality, twist it until you couldn't tell what was real and what was illusion. But this felt different. This felt like a call for help.

Without waiting for Kairos, Elera turned and ran toward the sound of her brother's voice, her heart racing. The trees seemed to close in around her as she sprinted through the forest, her feet pounding against the ground. Branches whipped against her face, but she barely noticed them. All she could hear was Seren's voice, growing louder with each step.

"Elera... help me..."

"Seren!" she called out, her voice desperate. "I'm coming!"

The trees thinned suddenly, and Elera stumbled into another clearing. The sight before her made her freeze in place.

Seren was there, standing in the middle of the clearing. He looked exactly as she remembered—his dark hair tousled, his eyes wide with fear. But there was something wrong. His form flickered, like a reflection on the surface of water, unstable and shifting.

"Elera," he said, his voice trembling. "You have to help me. I'm lost."

Elera's heart pounded in her chest as she took a step toward him. "Seren, what happened? How did you get here?"

"I don't know," Seren whispered, his voice filled with fear. "I tried to find you. I followed your path. But the shadow..."

Elera's blood ran cold. "The shadow? What do you mean?"

Seren's form flickered again, his face twisting with fear. "It's coming for me, Elera. It's going to take me."

Panic surged through Elera. She rushed forward, her hand outstretched. "No, I won't let it take you. I'll help you."

But just as her fingers were about to touch him, Seren's form flickered again, and his eyes filled with a dark, eerie light. The voice that spoke next wasn't Seren's.

"You can't save him, Elera."

Elera stumbled back, her heart hammering in her chest. The figure in front of her dissolved, the illusion shattering into a swirl of shadows that gathered at the edge of the clearing.

"You can't save him," the voice said again, deeper this time, echoing through the forest like a dark whisper. "You couldn't save anyone."

Elera's breath came in short gasps as the shadows closed in, swirling around her like a storm. The figure that had once been Seren was gone, replaced by a looming, dark presence that felt all too familiar.

The shadow.

"You're weak, Elera," the voice hissed. "You think you can fight me, but you can't. You've already failed."

Elera shook her head, her hands trembling as she clutched the moonstone in her pouch. "No," she whispered, her voice barely audible. "I haven't failed."

"You abandoned your brother," the shadow taunted, its voice cold and sharp. "You left him behind to chase after a power you don't even understand."

The words pierced through her, echoing the doubts she had carried since leaving her village. The shadow was feeding on her fear, twisting her memories, turning her own mind against her.

But then, a hand rested on her shoulder.

Kairos.

His presence was steady, grounding, pulling her out of the storm of doubt that threatened to consume her.

"Elera," he said softly, his voice cutting through the darkness. "It's not real. It's the Mirrorwood."

Elera looked up at him, her breath coming in ragged gasps. "I thought it was him," she whispered, tears stinging her eyes. "I thought Seren was here."

Kairos nodded, his expression filled with understanding. "The forest knows your fears. It's using them to break you. But you're stronger than this."

Elera swallowed hard, the weight of his words settling over her. The shadow was still there, lingering at the edge of her vision, but Kairos' presence gave her the strength to stand firm.

"You're right," she said, her voice steadier now. "It's not real."

The shadow hissed, its form flickering as it realized it was losing its grip on her. Elera clutched the moonstone, its pulse growing stronger in her hand, and took a step forward, her heart filled with renewed determination.

"You won't win," she said, her voice strong. "Not this time."

With a final, defiant roar, the shadow dissolved into the air, leaving behind only the quiet rustling of leaves in the breeze.

Chapter 20: The Light Beyond the Shadow

The sky above them was streaked with hues of violet and gold, the sun sinking low on the horizon, and the stars just beginning to shimmer faintly in the darkening sky. The moon hung high, a sliver of light against the deepening blue, watching over them like a silent guardian.

Elera glanced at Kairos as they walked, the soft glow of the moonstone pulsing gently in her pouch. He had been quieter than usual since they left the Mirrorwood, his brow furrowed in thought. She could feel the weight of the journey bearing down on both of them. There were still so many questions, so many uncertainties about the shadow, the moon's magic, and what awaited them beyond the peaks.

"Kairos," Elera began, her voice breaking the stillness, "what happens next? We've made it through the Mirrorwood, but the shadow is still out there. We haven't stopped it for good."

Kairos looked up at the sky, his expression thoughtful, but his voice was heavy with a burden he had yet to fully share. "The shadow was born from the moon's magic, twisted and corrupted over time. We've pushed it back, but the balance is still fragile. There's one more place we need to go."

Elera frowned. "Where?"

He pointed ahead, toward the horizon where the last light of the sun faded. "The Moonlit Pinnacle. It's the highest point in the Hidden Peaks, where the moon's power is strongest. The moonstone must be brought there. Only then can we ensure the shadow stays dormant."

The name sent a chill down Elera's spine. She had heard whispers of the Moonlit Pinnacle in legends, but she had never thought she would see it herself. It was said to be the place where the moon first cast its light on the earth, a sacred site where magic and reality intertwined. But it was also a place of great danger.

"The Moonlit Pinnacle," Elera repeated, her voice filled with both awe and apprehension. "Do you think we'll be able to stop the shadow once and for all?"

Kairos hesitated, his gaze distant. "I don't know. The shadow is tied to the moon's light. Even if we restore the balance, the darkness will always exist. But if we bring the moonstone to the Pinnacle, we can at least ensure that the shadow doesn't consume the light."

Elera nodded, though her heart felt heavy with uncertainty. They had come so far, and yet the final leg of their journey seemed more daunting than anything they had faced. The shadow, the darkness that had plagued them since the beginning, wasn't just an enemy to be fought—it was part of the magic itself, an inseparable force bound to the light.

As they climbed higher, the terrain became steeper, the air thinner. The path narrowed, winding between jagged rocks and cliffs that jutted out over deep ravines. But the moonstone's light continued to guide them, its soft glow growing stronger with each step, as if it knew they were nearing their destination.

After what felt like hours of climbing, they reached the base of the final ascent—a towering cliff that led up to the Moonlit Pinnacle. The path was treacherous, barely wide enough for one person at a time, with sheer drops on either side. The wind howled through the peaks, cold and sharp against their skin.

Kairos went first, his movements steady but careful, his eyes focused on the path ahead. Elera followed close behind, her heart pounding with both anticipation and fear. The moonstone in her pouch pulsed with a rhythmic beat, its light casting long shadows across the jagged rocks.

As they climbed, the wind seemed to carry whispers—faint, indistinct voices that echoed through the peaks. Elera's heart raced as she listened, but she couldn't make out the words. The voices were distant, like memories of an ancient past, carried on the wind from a time long forgotten.

Finally, after what felt like an eternity, they reached the top.

The Moonlit Pinnacle stretched out before them, a wide, flat expanse of stone bathed in the pale light of the moon. The air was crisp and clear, and the stars above seemed closer than ever, their light twinkling like distant fires. In the center of the Pinnacle was a circular platform, carved with intricate symbols that glowed faintly in the moonlight.

"This is it," Kairos said quietly, his voice barely audible over the wind. "This is where we make the final stand."

Elera stepped onto the platform, her heart racing. The moonstone in her pouch grew warm, its light intensifying until it was almost too bright to look at. She carefully pulled it out, the stone's glow casting long shadows across the Pinnacle.

For a moment, everything was still.

And then, from the shadows at the edge of the Pinnacle, something began to stir.

Elera's breath caught in her throat as the darkness gathered, swirling like smoke, twisting and writhing as it took form. The shadow was here—more powerful than ever. Its form shifted and flickered, tall and imposing, its eyes glowing with a cold, dark light.

"You cannot defeat me," the shadow hissed, its voice like the wind through the trees. "The light cannot exist without the darkness. You will fail."

Elera clenched the moonstone in her hand, its warmth spreading through her like a wave of calm. "We're not here to defeat you," she said, her voice steady. "We're here to restore the balance."

Kairos stepped forward, his sword drawn, his eyes locked on the shadow. "You've had your time in the dark," he said, his voice filled with quiet determination. "But the light belongs here too."

The shadow's form twisted, its shape flickering as it loomed closer. "You think you can keep me at bay?" it snarled, its voice filled with malice. "I am part of the magic. I am part of you."

Kairos' grip on his sword tightened, but Elera placed a hand on his arm, her eyes filled with resolve.

"We don't need to fight it, Kairos," she said softly. "We just need to let the light shine through."

She stepped forward, holding the moonstone high above her head. Its light blazed brighter than ever, filling the Pinnacle with a radiant glow that pushed back the shadows. The darkness writhed and twisted, trying to resist the light, but the moonstone's power was too strong.

The symbols on the platform beneath them began to glow, pulsing in rhythm with the moonstone's light. The wind howled around them, but Elera stood firm, her heart filled with a quiet, steady strength.

The shadow let out a final, furious roar, its form dissolving into the air as the light consumed it. The darkness faded, leaving behind only the soft glow of the moon and the stars.

Elera lowered the moonstone, her breath coming in short gasps. The shadow was gone—for now.

Kairos stood beside her, his expression unreadable, but there was a quiet peace in his eyes.

"We did it," Elera whispered, her voice trembling with both relief and exhaustion.

Kairos nodded, his gaze fixed on the horizon where the first light of dawn began to break. "The balance has been restored. But we'll need to protect it, always."

Elera smiled, the weight of the journey finally lifting from her shoulders. They had made it to the Moonlit Pinnacle, faced the shadow, and restored the light. The journey had been long and filled with trials, but together, they had found their way through the darkness.

And as the sun rose over the peaks, casting its golden light over the land, Elera knew that this wasn't the end.

It was a new beginning.
THE END